RUSTLER ON THE BEACH

Other books by the same author

RUSTLER ON THE BEACH

A Novel of Adventure
and Romance

FRANK MULVILLE

Angus and Robertson•Publishers

ANGUS AND ROBERTSON

London · Sydney · Melbourne · Singapore · Manila

First published by Angus and Robertson (U.K.) Ltd. 1976

Copyright © Frank Mulville 1976

ISBN 0 207 95656 1

Made and printed in Great Britain by
Northumberland Press Limited
Gateshead

ONE

Julie once said to me, 'You know, Sam, you love the *Rustler* better than you love me. If you had to choose between us, you'd choose her.'

She didn't say it with bitterness—she was never jealous of the *Rustler*, she loved her as much as I did myself. She stated it as a matter of fact which she accepted as part of the order of things. I denied it, but it was true—I knew it was true. The *Rustler* was mine, my own thing, as if I had created her. She had been a part of me for as long as I could remember, since I was a small boy. Not the *Rustler* herself, it is true, but the idea of her, the vision of her. She was warm, she was beautiful, she responded to my moods, whispering comfort to me with the music that came from her slender bow as it parted the waters. She could be obstinate, she could be heavy and awkward, she could be perverse, but we always understood one another. I loved her when she threshed into the wind, smiting the steep waves of the English Channel and sending the crystal spray stinging across the deck. I loved her when a strong quartering wind made her twist and rear and romp as I checked her mad careering with the wheel. I loved her in the night when the masthead swung against the Milky Way, describing great sweeps across the bowl of the sky. She was mine, you see. All mine. Her song was my sweetest music.

I started the boat fund when I was twelve, when my mother died. I suppose I conceived it as some sort of compensation, something that would put back what had been taken away.

My brothers and my sister were older. My sister was already married when Mother died and had already gone out of my life. One of my brothers had been killed two years before in a mining accident and the other went off to sea. He would occasionally come back to the house in Newhaven where I lived with Dad and then he would be off again, perhaps for a year, perhaps for a month. To me he was a strange, romantic figure coming and going unpredictably.

We lived in a terraced council house. Dad was a fitter in the power station. We were what they call good working-class stock. Dad never married again and the two of us lived alone in the house. When I was at school Dad would do the shopping on his way to work and he would cook the evening meal when he came home at night. In the school holidays I did the shopping and sometimes I would cook the meal as well, to give him a surprise. He had a passion for music and he spent all his spare money on records, and books about famous composers, an odd taste for a working man. I suppose he was something of an eccentric. He had a powerful amplifier with two huge speakers, and he would fill the house in the evenings with sound so that the little living room seemed to palpitate like a heart, swelling and contracting with the music.

Sharp at ten o'clock the neighbours would hammer on the wall and we would stop it and go to bed. If they hammered in the middle of one of his favourite pieces, he would swear, 'Ignorant buggers', and then he would be in a bad temper the next day. Dad seldom spoke about Mother but when he did, it was as if she was still there in the house. 'Don't do that Sam,' he would say. 'You'll upset your mother.' About once a month he would go out and get drunk—something he never did before she died. He would come back after the pub chucked him out, walking very carefully and very straight, holding himself stiff like a soldier. All he would say was, 'It's all right Sam, I'm drunk,' and then he would go to bed. It used to scare me a bit.

Our road was a dead end and we only had neighbours on

6

one side. The other side of the house was a high blank wall with a factory behind it. The Evans' never minded the music —they referred to it as 'the noise'—provided it stopped sharp at ten. If it didn't, Mr Evans would be round thundering on the front door. It wasn't a bad life but the strangeness of it made it difficult for me to make friends of my own age—made me into something of a loner. At first I used to think about Mother a good bit. Sometimes the tears would just come, but as time passed she began to fade into a sort of nostalgic cloud which I could visit when I was alone. Mother had an all-embracing love for all of us—I think she loved everyone in the whole world. She was always the same, tolerant, calm, un-hurried, sympathetic. She wasn't an exceptional person in any way, not talented or gifted although she had educated herself. She was a great reader. But she was there, and when she died of cancer she left a cruel hole.

The boat fund started in an old tin the day Mother died. My brother Dick gave me five bob that day and I put half a crown of it in the bottom of a coffee tin. I had a proper money box, as all children do, but the boat fund was something different and separate. Twenty years later, when I bought the *Rustler*, I put that half crown under the mast step. I don't think I was miserly about money. I spent it when I got it on sweets, or the pictures or anything I wanted like any other boy, but whenever I had any extra, I always put something in the tin. When it got full I started a savings account in the Post Office. I never told a soul about it. Dad was quite generous with pocket money and he'd often say, 'Keep the change Sam,' after I had done the shopping. When Dick came home he was always good for ten bob and sometimes I did odd jobs round the harbour to bump the boat fund a bit. I found a fiver one day, lying on the ground near the harbour, all folded up and looking like a piece of waste paper. Once I stole a pound from out of the till in the grocer's. I lifted it when the girl wasn't look-ing. I hated that pound—I couldn't put it in the boat fund because of Mother.

7

I spent most of my time round the harbour. Even before Mother died I was a bit of a harbour urchin, sailing toy boats at high tide when the sea came in over the saltings, getting covered in mud and talking to the workmen in Mr Pell's boat-yard. It was a small yard—slipping, repairs, fitting out and that sort of thing. They used to build small cruising boats. They always built one in the winter and in this way they could keep their men employed all the year round. Mr Pell inherited the yard from his father who had started it years ago, round the turn of the century. He took quite a fancy to me, he had no son of his own, only two daughters and he never minded me hanging about the yard. He had an odd habit of always saying 'or something' at the end of a sentence as if he was never quite sure of himself.

After Mother died I began to go to the yard more and more. I got to know all the men, did odd jobs, sometimes made a couple of bob that way for the fund. I used to make the tea for the men's elevenses and I used to help on boat repairing and boat building jobs, passing up tools and running errands. I absorbed knowledge through my skin as boys do. Occasionally during the holidays I would get a day out with one of the fishermen, and once or twice I managed to get a trip across to Dieppe on one of the cross-Channel boats without anyone knowing that I was on board.

Mr Pell used to let me use one of the yard's boats. She was a heavy old skiff and had once been a barge's dinghy. One of the men in the yard found a mast and an old lug for her and I used to scull her out of the harbour and sail her out to sea off Beachy Head, steering with an oar over the stern. I had some adventures in that old boat. She taught me how to sail and how to use the tides and how to watch the weather and how to work up to wind'ard with an old lug without a centre board. Sometimes I would be out all day and half the night trying to get back against the flood tide. I once sailed her round the Royal Sovereign Light Vessel and back again, but I copped it from Dad when I got home, half starved, at eleven o'clock at night. All in all it wasn't a bad childhood, though I must have been an odd little boy. It meant that I grew up quickly. I was a man by the time I was sixteen.

One day in Mr Pell's yard I met a man who changed my life. His name was Cranbrook. He was a rich man, a gentleman, and at the same time he was a cultivated man. Mr Cranbrook was nothing of a snob—he hadn't a bit of side on him. He was a director of some big business in London and he owned a boat called the *Maydew*—a big, expensive, bermudian cutter, almost new.

The *Maydew* had come into Newhaven the previous week-end. Mr Pell told me they had left her for the week in the yard for some minor repairs and were going to take her round to Cowes the following Friday. I had just finished school and was filling in time at the yard until I could get a job. I sculled out in the skiff a couple of times and had a good look at the *Maydew*. I was working on the jetty on Thursday, painting one of the yard boats and whistling an air from a Mozart opera— my head was full of it. It was as familiar to me as 'pop'. Mr Cranbrook asked me to row him out to the *Maydew*. On the way he quizzed me about the music.

'Where did you pick that up?' he asked.

'I get it from Dad—all day long.'

He asked me on board and showed me round. I had never been aboard anything so magnificent. She was a beauty. She had everything you could want for running the ship, but nothing unnecessary. She was tidy and workmanlike on deck, comfort- able and simple below. Mr Cranbrook told me the *Maydew* was going off on an ocean race soon, but she was one man short as someone had cried off at the last minute. Would I like to go? I ran all the way home, left a note for Dad, then ran all the way back with a kit-bag of gear.

We lay for the night in the outer harbour, through the swing bridge with just Mr Cranbrook and me on board. The rest of the crew came down the next morning, which was Friday. Mr Cranbrook dragged out of me everything about my life—about Dad, Mum dying, the music and the two of us living alone and looking after ourselves. I told him I had just packed up school and was looking for a job.

There was plenty to do on board to get the *Maydew* ready for a race—bending on sails, checking gear, stowing away the stores and setting out the charts and sailing directions. It was one of the short ocean races, from Cowes out across the Channel and back round the Isle of Wight. We were to leave Newhaven as soon as the crew joined and sail to the Solent, to be on the starting line at eleven on Saturday morning. Mr Cranbrook sent me ashore with a ten-pound note to buy some forgotten stores—pretty trusting of him I thought as he'd only known me for a few hours. I cooked supper for the two of us and we turned in early, me in a pipe-cot in the fo'castle and Mr Cranbrook in the saloon. It felt pretty good lying in that cot. I felt as if I had lived for a day as I had never lived before. I could hear the water slip-slopping against the hull, the light tap of a rope against the mast. I could feel the boat moving gently against the quay, straining against her mooring ropes and creaking gently. The fo'castle was a treasure store, with a shaft of silver moon filtering through coils of rope, hanks of twine, spare sails, an oil lamp swinging from the deck head, flares, a pair of rowlocks, signal flags, an old brass foghorn on the bulkhead. I could smell the smell of boat, thick and turgid like an exotic soup.

The rest of the crew came in a big black car soon after Mr Cranbrook and I had finished breakfast. The chauffeur was told to pick us up in Southampton, on Sunday evening.

Mr Cranbrook introduced me, 'This is my daughter Julie— Sam Pickson—my sons John, Robert.'

The boys said, 'Hello, Sam,' and Julie looked at me and smiled. She was about my age—a tall, thin girl with striking brown eyes—great big round eyes—one of them had a segment of a much lighter brown in the iris. She was spotty and not very attractive, not the sort of girl to rave about.

By way of explanation Mr Cranbrook said, 'I met Sam at

Mr Pell's yard yesterday and he agreed to come in place of Simon.'

Julie made coffee for us all and we left harbour immediately to catch the tide along the coast. I could tell from the first moment that Mr Cranbrook was a first-class skipper. The boys were experienced and knew exactly what to do with no more than a nod or a quietly spoken word. We stopped the engine as soon as we were clear of the harbour entrance and hoisted sail. It was sunny with a brisk north-easterly which sent us bowling along the coast.

I shall never forget that day. It was the first time I had been sailing in a boat of any size or any quality and it made a profound impression. It was one of those clear, bright spring days when the world seems cast out of crystal, the sea bubbling champagne, the shore-line standing across the horizon like a page from a child's painting book, white cliffs covered with gaudy green, toy lighthouses and towns with piers and domes and steeples. I felt awake and aware as I had never felt before. The *Maydew* ran at eight, sometimes nine knots, a quartering wind blowing off the shore, each tiny wave with a crest of white, gulls veering and banking across the stern, the wake knitting the sea into an even pattern. We set her mains'l and a huge genoa, a vast white bosom of a sail. The sheets and stays were bar tight and singing with strain. I worked with John and Robert as if I had been doing it all my life—it seemed to come naturally to me—the skill I needed had been with me always, only waiting to be used. Mr Cranbrook was pleased.

'You've done this before,' he said. 'Here, come and take her.'

To take the wheel was to feel the pulse of this fine ship. She responded like a girl to a caress—quick and eager and anxious to please yet firm to touch. She was a live creature, strong, impulsive but disciplined. I felt like a king.

We covered the sixty odd miles from Newhaven to Cowes in nine hours and tied up alongside the pontoons in the Medina River before nightfall. Mr Cranbrook and the two boys went off ashore to some yacht club, Julie and I stayed on board and cooked scrambled eggs for supper. I was glad not to go ashore as I felt uneasy with John and Robert—they were like people from another world. They spoke a different language and they talked about things I had no knowledge of. John was at university studying economics or some such thing and Robert, the elder, worked in Mr Cranbrook's business. They were civil and polite but I knew that what went on their world was no business of mine and what went on in my world was of no interest to them. Julie was different—I think she was more like her father. She asked me a lot of questions and told me about herself. She was going to leave school, go to college and be an actress.

'You mean on the box?' I asked her.

'Well, maybe—but I want to be in the theatre—the real theatre—you know, out on the stage in front of people.'

'I couldn't get on with school,' I said. 'I've packed it up. I'm going to get a job—buy a boat some day—but not like this one I don't suppose.' I looked round ruefully at the *Maydew*—she must be worth thousands, a sum of money altogether beyond my understanding. 'Unless I win the pools or rob a bank.'

'Do you do the pools?'

'No.'

'That means the bank, then.'

'Don't be silly—I was joking.'

The others came back late—I was already in my bunk in the fo'castle—keyed up, excited and wide awake. Julie was asleep I think. I heard Mr Cranbrook say in a sort of tired, disillusioned voice, 'Better turn in and get some sleep—we've all got a long day tomorrow.'

The other two were having some sort of argument: Robert seemed angry. 'You're a bloody idiot to dope yourself up just before a race—what sort of a state are you going to be in tomorrow? You'll be awake all night and sleep all day. A great help. What the hell do you think that boy'll make of you? Bloody unfair.'

12

'Take it easy, keep calm, relax,' John replied. 'You don't have to worry about the peasantry.'

His voice was slurred and thick and supercilious. Pot probably—I'd seen plenty of kids in that state in Brighton. I despised John from that moment on—a remark like that sticks. I knew he meant it. Mr Cranbrook had never spoken a word to me that didn't come as if from an equal to an equal in spite of the gulf between me and him—age, class, wealth, education, everything. I felt hurt and sorry for him. He didn't deserve a son like that. I went to sleep with the sticky, thick smell of marijuana hanging round the boat like a sick cloud.

I forgot about John the next morning—he spent most of the day in his bunk and I hardly saw him until the afternoon. The excitement was intense and the impressions crowded in one on top of the next. I didn't have room in my head for anything except the job of working the ship. Robert and I did the work and Mr Cranbrook steered and gave orders in his quiet voice. Twenty big ocean racers jostling for position on the starting line in a fresh easterly breeze—what a sight. They were everywhere, going in every direction, each one striving for advantage between the ten-minute gun and the start. The noise of the great genoas shaking in the wind, the rattle of the sheet winches, an occasional shout of 'starboard', or 'water', as one massive sailing machine tried to crowd another out of position. Then the gun went and suddenly the chaos was resolved into order. The boats spread out across the Solent in an uneven line, the coloured spinnakers opened like flowers, the bow waves curled up under twenty slim forefoots and the tranquil shores of the Isle of Wight began to slip away. *Maydew* was third across the line and a lucky gust gave her the lead off Yarmouth. Through the Needles Channel the fleet was behind us, a pack of white hounds on the run out to sea.

On the way down Channel the yachts spread out. We kept in front, there were two or three close on our tail but we soon lost the bulk of them. *Maydew* was one of the biggest in the fleet and one of the fastest. Mr Cranbrook handed over the wheel to Robert and went below to work out the course to the Shambles Light Vessel, forty miles down Channel. He set the watches, two hours on the helm and four hours off for Robert and I and John, who had come to life looking a bit washed out—Julie to do the cooking and help with sail changing when necessary. Mr Cranbrook did not take a watch but he was always about. He never seemed to sleep except for a few minutes at a time, and he kept a constant eye on the weather, the wind and the course, and was always the first to sense the need for some change in trim or some advantage that might be gained from a slight variation in the course. We were short-handed, there ought to have been two on deck together but Mr Cranbrook didn't mind.

'Better to have five people who know what they're doing than a lot of amateurs tumbling over each other.'

I took the remark as something of a compliment. John, Robert and Julie certainly knew what they were doing. What I knew about sailing I had learned from Mr Pell's old skiff and from books, but I was new to the disciplined routine of a large, efficient yacht.

At nightfall we rounded the Shambles and turned on the wind. As it freshened, the big genoa was changed for a high cut jib and *Maydew* buried her lee rail and began to race to wind'ard. The sense of power was overwhelming as she forced her way forward against the wind and through the seas. Every rope and wire and terylene sail was bar tight. She would shudder as she took a sea over the bow, water and stinging spray would sweep across the deck, battering against the dodgers that protected the helmsman, hissing and spitting like a thousand demons. Below, the motion took on an insane violence, the whole cabin shaking and bucking and sweeping through every variety of movement. It was like lying inside a football on cup final day. Julie spent her time wedged in a corner on the lee bunk, her feet braced against the motion, reading a book—it was Shaw's *Pygmalion*. She made us hot soup and endless cups of tea and could always find a meal for anyone who was hungry.

Steering took all my concentration. Mr Cranbrook showed me how to watch the movement of the ship and the shape and size of the seas, how to nurse the boat through the ever changing complexity of ocean that surrounded her, how to watch the instruments and to keep the boat as close to the wind as she would sail, never pinching, never allowing her to fall off, always easing her and giving to her, but always firmly guiding her to her purpose. The clouds scudded across the windy stars, *Maydew* reared and plunged and cut a swathe through the boiling sea, the log read eight and a half knots and I was in my seventh heaven.

We won the race easily, finishing first and saving our handicap. We tied up alongside the pontoon in Cowes, Julie cooked us a meal and we all went ashore to the club. It was a posh place. I had never been anywhere like it before. It was full of young men dressed in blue blazers and club ties and sleek girls in well-cut trousers and expensive sweaters. I nursed a pint of bitter and kept myself as much out of the way as I could.

The two boys and Julie soon met up with friends—I noticed that John disappeared with a friend almost as soon as we arrived. Mr Cranbrook was talking to the owner of one of the other yachts in the race.

'This is Sam Pickson,' he introduced me round. 'I met him by chance in Newhaven. Says he's never been racing before but he seems to know a hell of a lot. I think he'll make one of the best crews I've ever had.'

He talked about the race for a time, then the conversation passed on to things I didn't understand—business, the Stock Exchange, interest rates, 'going public' and 'liquidity'. I slipped away and found a quiet corner from where I could watch, and after a time I found Julie beside me.

'What do you make of all this, Sam?'

'Well, I suppose it's all right. I'm not used to people like this, makes me feel a bit strange.'

'I think they're dreadful,' she said, looking at me with her round, brown eyes. 'I can't stand any of them. Not an ounce of

15

grey matter among the lot. Stuffed, that's what they are. I only come because Father likes me to, and because I love the boat and the sailing.'

Soon Mr Cranbrook was gathering us together. 'Time to catch the ferry. Where's John?'

Robert looked round the room for a minute. 'Oh Christ, I know where he'll be, I'll get him.'

He disappeared and came back with John behind him. John looked a bit unsteady and had the glazed look which must have been familiar to Mr Cranbrook. He looked hard at him, but said nothing.

We caught the ferry. The big, black car was waiting at Southampton, the chauffeur dozing in the front seat.

'Drive to Newhaven first,' Mr Cranbrook said. 'We'll drop Sam and then go on to London. It's not far out of our way.'

I was sitting in the front but I heard John, in the back, say, 'Can't he get a bus or hitch or something?'

'Shut up,' Mr Cranbrook said.

Jubilee Street was quiet. A stray dog sat staring at nothing in the middle of the road. Scrawled on the blank wall at the end were the words, 'Blacks—Go home' and underneath it, 'God forgot this place'. The houses were old and run down—it was Queen Victoria's jubilee, not King George's.

Our house was number sixty-four. A faint light showed behind the curtains, you could hear Mozart clearly from the street. It was the statue music from *Don Giovanni*.

Mr Cranbrook said, 'Cheerio Sam—thanks a lot—I'll drop you a line,' and then the big black car turned round in our street and was gone.

TWO

I was always shy and hesitant about girls—even secretive. I once had an affair with a girl I met at a dance in Newhaven—I fell in love with her and wanted to marry her. Her background was working class, but her family had come up in the world. Her father worked in a bank and they lived in a solid, middle-class house on the outskirts of the town. When her parents found out that we lived in Jubilee Street, the whole thing fell through. It was a bit of a shock to me and I made up my mind never again to mix in a class I didn't belong to. This was long after I had finished, or thought I had finished with Mr Cranbrook and his family.

That first weekend in the *Maydew* set my mind in turmoil. After it, there was no possible doubt that I had to have a boat. I had to get money and I had to have a boat. It wouldn't be anything like the *Maydew*, I knew that, I didn't even want it to be. I had been reading books about boats for years. I had seen hundreds of boats, not only in Newhaven but in Hamble where I often used to go on the bus on a Saturday. Gradually the picture began to form in my mind of the boat I knew I would have one day. She would not be a racer like the *Maydew*. I hadn't the slightest interest in racing and I agreed with Julie about racing people. No, she would be a gaff cutter or maybe a gaff yawl. Not too big, something I could handle myself or with one other person. She would be old and cheap and I would work on her and do her up and make her strong and seaworthy. I would learn how to navigate from books and then I would set off—go foreign as my brother Dick would say. She was all there in my mind's eye. All I had to do was to get money and I reckoned that over a few years I'd do it. When Mr Cranbrook sent me five pounds it brought the boat fund up to one hundred pounds. Well, it was a start.

The five pounds came on the Wednesday after that first weekend. There was a brief note with it, written on smart, blue letterheading with Consolidated Finance Limited embossed in red. 'Dear Sam, if you can manage it I'd like you to come again in two weeks' time. The car will call for you on Friday at eleven a.m. unless you let me know to the contrary. Regards, Roger Cranbrook.' There was no mention of the fiver, it was just there in the envelope folded in half.

I was already working in my first job; I had been to the Labour Exchange and got a job on a construction site. I was a hefty lad and the foreman took me on straightaway. I didn't mind the work, in fact I liked it. The money was good and I didn't kill myself although I worked long hours—eight in the morning until six at night, and all day Saturday. Nobody seemed to worry if I took a couple of days off. In fact, nobody worried about me at all—they just took me at face value and didn't ask questions. That suited me fine. Dad was pleased as it meant money coming into the house. He would have liked me to have stayed at school to get a posh job in an office but that didn't fit in with my plans.

Sharp at eleven on the Friday following, the black car rolled up outside our house, with just the chauffeur in it, and we drove to Southampton where I got the ferry to Cowes. The weekend was much the same as the first one except that I was more familiar with the boat and the gear, and more at ease with Julie and her brothers. I never made real friends with Robert or John, except in a casual way. Robert was a bit superior and I had no doubt about John's attitude towards me but I didn't mind. He smoked pot a good deal. I could see that Mr Cranbrook hated John's habit but I never heard him say a word. Maybe he thought it would pass and that anyway it didn't do John much harm.

I suppose I went sailing with them half a dozen times that first season and more often the next. They took me on a cruise to Brittany with them for a fortnight. Julie was always friendly and pleasant. I never saw Mrs Cranbrook and they didn't talk about her much. I gathered she was a bit of an invalid. She didn't like boating and she never came on board the *Maydew*.

I came to respect Mr Cranbrook more and more as I knew him better. He used to talk to me about music—he knew a lot about it, much more than I did—and about books. He got me on to reading all sorts of stuff—politics, philosophy, economics, history—books that I had never considered before. Reading came easily to me, perhaps I had picked up the habit from Mother. They never met Dad and never came into the house although most of the weekends I spent with them, the black car would pick me up and drop me at home again. Mr Cranbrook wanted me to go to night school and get some qualifications. 'Something you can get your teeth into, Sam. Make something interesting out of your life. You can't spend the rest of your days labouring on a building site.'

I knew exactly what I wanted to do, although I didn't say anything to Mr Cranbrook, or to anyone else, and the labouring suited my purpose perfectly. I earned good money and I stowed it away in the boat fund. The post office book got full and I started a deposit account in a bank.

For a long time life went on much as usual at number sixty-four Jubilee Street. I graduated from labouring to driving a bulldozer and I began to get jobs in other parts of the country. I got myself a motorbike so I could come home as often as possible—I didn't like leaving Dad for too long. He was getting on a bit, near retiring age, and as he grew older he became more eccentric. The house was so full of records you could hardly get in: records in piles all over the floor in the tiny living room, records on every table, every shelf, every flat surface, even on the kitchen dresser. He began to neglect himself a bit, too, coming in from work and sitting in his chair with the music, without eating or even making himself a cup of tea until ten o'clock when Mr Evans would hammer on the wall. Then the music would stop and he would get himself some bread and cheese and stump off to bed. 'It reminds me of your mother', he said to me one day, 'Seems to bring her back to me—I can't do without it'. He would go to the pub every Saturday now, coming back erect and dignified and blind drunk. 'Don't take any notice of me, Sam—I'm drunk.' I believe he said it whether I was there or not.

My brother Dick would blow in from the sea every now and then. Sometimes I was there and sometimes I wasn't but once, near the end, I saw him and he said, 'You know, Sam, Dad's going potty—he's near round the bend. What are you going to do about it?'

'Nothing,' I said. 'He's happy—leave him be.'

After a couple of seasons sailing in the *Maydew* I lost touch with the Cranbrooks. I never heard from them and the black car stopped coming. I always used to go down to the yard when I was home and have a yarn with Mr Pell and have a look at the boats in the yard. I believe Mr Pell knew what I was after and I believe he knew the sort of boat I wanted.

One day he said to me, 'The *Maydew* was in here last week Sam—new owner or something. They told me the previous owner—Cranbrook, wasn't it?—has gone abroad—Australia or something. They said his business crashed, or something.'

I was curious so I telephoned the number on the Consolidated Finance letterheading.

'Consolidated Finance?' the girl said. 'They left here a couple of years ago—went broke, I believe.'

I was sorry for Mr Cranbrook but I guessed he had more than likely come out of it all right. He had always seemed to me so immensely rich that I could not imagine a state of affairs in which he was without funds. Anyway, I was grateful to him for the help he had given me. Since he had started me off reading all those books I had formed some pretty definite ideas about life. I had glimpsed it from the top on those brief spells in the *Maydew* and I had seen it from the bottom. I wasn't complaining—I only had myself to look after—I worked hard and earned good money but I knew a lot who worked hard and went short and I had seen a few who, it seemed to me, did precious little and had it to burn. I never had anything to do with politics. I wasn't that interested. I knew what I wanted out of life and I didn't much mind what anyone else thought. I listened to them all—some of the shop stewards were pretty militant and dragged us out on strike a few times. I had to admit we usually got something out of it. The Marxists were the most interesting—they wanted to bust the whole business open and start again. When I looked around me it didn't seem such a bad idea.

My brother Dick wanted me to go to sea. 'Earn good money, see the world. You're crazy about boats, Sam, you'd like it.'

I might have done if it hadn't been for Dad, but I didn't see I could leave him alone. He had no one else in the world except me—we never heard from my sister year in and year out. I wasn't even sure of her address. I thought it would hit Dad hard if I went off, and, anyway, I was enjoying life in my own way. As the years passed I began to take an interest in all sorts of odd things—the theatre, old buildings, picture galleries, and of course, concerts. I was a complete square I suppose and it put me right out on a limb—rather as I had been as a boy. I could never mention any of these things to my mates—most of them would have thought I was daft.

I did meet a girl I fell for once—the one whose father worked in a bank—but the whole affair left me with a sick feeling inside, a feeling of being somehow apart. I never formed any deep attachments after that—I had plenty of girls but it was always on a strictly business basis for me.

Dad had never been to a concert in his life. He had never even seen an orchestra, so one Saturday I booked two seats in the front row of the circle at the Festival Hall and took him to London in a taxi. He hadn't been to London since Mother died ten years previously. He was like a child at the circus for the first time. He watched wide-eyed as the orchestra filed in, took their seats and began to tune their instruments and then, when the programme started I had a job to keep him in his seat. Dad wanted to get up and conduct. The music was completely familiar to him—he knew it backwards and he had his own ideas of how it should be played. I don't think he had ever associated together in his mind the idea of music and the thought of people actually performing it. He was quite unimpressed by the solemn dignity of the Festival Hall, shouting out and waving his arms wildly. People round us were sucking their teeth and saying, 'Shhh....' and in the interval an usher came up to our seats and said, 'I'm sorry sir—you'll have to be quiet or leave the hall'. I was glad when it was over and I think Dad was too. It had been a traumatic experience for him. In the foyer on the way out I left him for a moment. 'Wait right here, Dad, while I get the coats.' When I came back there was a tall girl standing near him. I don't think I would have recognized her, it was ten years since I had seen her. Her face and her body had filled out, the thin, spotty look had gone. Rich brown hair hung over her shoulders curling under in a roll, her lips were full and red, she was pale with a touch of colour over her cheekbones. But when she turned towards me it was unmistakable—the fleck of light brown in her right eye made her face unique and unforgettable. She was with another couple—they were all in evening dress. Julie was wearing a dark crimson velvet dress with long sleeves and a high, round neck, absolutely plain. She looked beautiful. She saw me and I noticed a look of perplexed uncertainty in her eyes for a split second, and then sudden recognition. It was like watching clouds racing across the sun. 'Sam—hello—how wonderful to see you—how are you?'

I was caught off balance; I was like a schoolboy blushing and stammering and scared stiff.

'I'm fine, I'm with my Dad—got a taxi waiting—ought to go really—it's a bit late for Dad.'

She turned her back on her friends, and looked at me with her big round eyes. 'Sam, I'd love to have a chat sometime—

find out how you're getting on—why not look me up? Arts Theatre Club, London. They always know where I can be found.'

I said, 'Why, yes, that's fine. I'll look you up sometime,' and fled, dragging Dad behind me.

Dad didn't say anything during the long taxi ride back home and he never mentioned the concert afterwards, not once. I never again heard him play records of the Mozart, the Strauss or the Schubert that we had heard.

The boat fund grew slowly but surely year by year. By the time I was twenty-six I had nearly five thousand pounds saved up—a hell of a big sum of money to me. I began to look in earnest for a boat. I began to buy the yachting magazines and then to go round on my motorbike on Sundays looking at boats I had seen advertised. I saw dozens all along the south coast and even up as far as Burnham. Most of them were hopeless; one look was enough to tell me I was wasting my time. A few were possible, but I always found that if they were sound and in good condition they were too expensive for me and if they were cheap they were rotten. I wanted a wooden boat, not plastic. I knew what to look for: rot in the deck beams or the covering boards, cracked timbers, soft beam shelf, perished keel bolts, decaying rudder trunks. I probed with my penknife like a surgeon in search of a cancer and more often than not the blade sank in to the hilt and a bubble of moisture formed as I withdrew it. It wasn't easy to find a sound, wooden boat at the right price. Then one Saturday I got talking to Mr Pell in the yard.

'Sam,' he said, 'there's a boat lying in the mud—came in last week or something—take the skiff and go'n have a look.'

It was the top of a spring tide, one of those still, autumn days. The *Rustler* was riding high over the saltings, looking like a model set in a glass sea. She was a gaff yawl of about twelve tons—very run-down she looked. Her spars hadn't seen a coat of varnish for years, her wood blocks were blackened with the weather, her cordage looked as if it was on its last legs and rusty scars from the chain plates disfigured her topsides.

I took in her lines at a glance—a spoon bow, high and power-ful, a very sweet sheer, low coach roof and a smooth run aft to a canoe stern. Some misguided owner had built an ugly doghouse over her cockpit but if you looked at her and imagined that the doghouse wasn't there, you could see that she was a remarkably pretty boat. Her sails had been carelessly furled and bundled up untidily with a few tyers. I sculled the skiff all round her and looked at her from every angle. Her powerful bow was matched by strong quarters and a solid aft section. She had bulwarks all round, a short bowsprit and a bumkin over the stern. There was a porthole or a glass deadlight let into the topsides on the port side in way of the mast—but nothing to match it on the other side. She wouldn't fly, I thought, but she'd be a friend in a gale of wind. I went on board. She was a real mess with gear lying in heaps all over the coach roof, the varnish peeling off her hatches and an air of careless neglect about her but her decks seemed sound as did the mast and spars. The companionway was locked with a big brass padlock but the forehatch had been carelessly left open and I went below. She was gloomy with mess everywhere, but you could see that she must have been a lovely boat in her heyday. The saloon was big, with a mahogany table down the centre. For'ard on the port side there was a separate cabin—a large bunk with drawers under and a tip-up wash basin. The deadlight was just at the head of the bunk. On the other side of the ship was the galley and the lavatory separated by a bulkhead. The fo'castle was small but cosy. I couldn't find much wrong with her. I had a funny feeling inside as I sculled ashore.

Mr Pell said, 'The owner told me he was selling her. Said his wife was ill and he couldn't manage her any more—or something. Didn't tell me how much he wanted for her but you could write to him if you like.'

He gave me an address in Leeds and I wrote off the same night. The reply came within a few days. 'Dear Mr Pickson, it is correct that I am anxious to sell the *Rustler*. The price asked is £7,000 but I would take £6,000 for a quick cash sale.'

I wrote back equally briefly. 'Dear Mr Johnson, I am sorry, the price asked for the *Rustler* is more money than I have. I could only give you £4,000. I have the money available for immediate payment.'

There was no reply.

I realized that I wanted the *Rustler*, I wanted her badly. I got Mr Pell to come on board with me the following Saturday and we went over her together. Mr Pell found a soft place up under her stern but he reckoned it was nothing much. We looked at her bottom, as much as we could see of her at low tide, but we couldn't find much wrong. Her engine was in poor shape but there was nothing wrong with it except rust and dirt and neglect. She was in a filthy state, but sound as far as we could see.

Mr Pell said, 'She's probably worth what he's asking, Sam— there's nothing much wrong with her that a bit of hard work won't put right.'

A week later Dad died. I was working on a site near home, earning good money clearing away for the foundations of a block of flats. Dad was already home when I arrived on the Thursday evening. I made our supper and we sat quietly eating it as we always did, then I left him to do the washing up, changed and went off to Brighton on the motorbike. I was going for a special purpose—'Back about eleven,' and I was gone. I often went to the theatre in Brighton and when there was anything good on I made a point of going. This time it was *Pygmalion*—I had seen it advertised in the paper—and playing the part of Eliza Doolittle was Julie Cranbrook. It was nearly two years since I had met her in London and I hadn't seen her since. I had often thought of leaving a message for her, as she had suggested, and arranging to meet her, but then when I thought about it again, I realized it was no good. Julie and I couldn't have anything in common, except sailing, and I had no boat anyway. Julie was the sort of girlfriend I could never have, as a friend or anything else. I had tried it before and had sworn never to do it again.

It wasn't a bad performance of *Pygmalion* and Julie was good as Eliza—brilliant, I thought. I stood outside the theatre for five minutes trying to decide whether to go round to the stage door and make myself known—then I made up my mind and rode off home. Maybe I'd go again if she was on next week. Perhaps it would be nice to talk to her for half an hour. I wanted to know what had happened to Mr Cranbrook.

When I got back to Jubilee Street it was quarter to eleven. I heard the music thundering out before I ever stopped the bike—it was the Brahms No. 2 Piano Concerto and at once I knew something was wrong. Evans was hammering on the front door.

'The noise—he won't stop it,' he said to me, angrily.

'I'm sorry Mr Evans—I'll see it's put off right away.'

He went back into his house muttering. I let myself in with my key. The light was on—everything was exactly as it always was, Dad sitting in his chair, the washing-up all done, the music on loud—but Dad was already stiff. I was so dumbfounded I just stood there looking at him. I didn't even switch off the music until Evans, hammering on the wall, brought me to my senses. Poor old Dad—oh Christ—what the hell was I going to do now. There was no one. I was alone except for Dick, wherever he might be. I realized suddenly how fond I had been of Dad. He was someone to look after, someone who needed me, someone I didn't have to keep secrets from. Suddenly life seemed a hell of a drag.

I didn't know what to do. For a long time I just stood there listening to the clock ticking and looking at Dad, sitting there with his eyes closed as if he was asleep, but quite white. It didn't seem possible he would never wake up. After about an hour I went out, tiptoeing so as not to disturb him maybe, walked down to the corner and telephoned the doctor. A woman answered.

'It's my Dad,' I said. 'He's dead.'

26

'Natural causes?' she asked.

'Yes—natural causes—that's it—natural causes.'

'Please leave your name and address. The doctor will call as soon as possible.' I went home and made a cup of tea.

'Natural—yes, I suppose it's quite natural.'

I waited. In about two hours a young doctor arrived and examined Dad.

'Heart failure—natural causes—you can call in for the death certificate tomorrow.'

I went through all the routine—it wasn't difficult. Three men in bowler hats came and took Dad to the morgue. The cremation was fixed for the next day, all very quick and businesslike. There were no mourners, no flowers, no one there except me and I went to the crematorium on my motorbike. I had to insist that no religion came into it—no ashes to ashes and dust to dust and all that stuff. Dad had always said he wanted it that way. 'I've never had anything to do with religion,' he used to say, 'and I don't want it when I die. Just shove me in the fire and say cheerio,' and that's what I said, 'Cheerio Dad.'

I didn't know what to do with myself for the next couple of weeks. I was lonely, really lonely. I had never been lonely before even when I was away from home because I always knew Dad was there. The knowledge that he was there made it all right. It wasn't even that we talked a lot or shared a lot of common interests, it was just that he was there. I kept looking at the *Rustler* and wondering if I could raise enough money to buy her. Dad left next to nothing—£100 in the Post Office and the records. I kept thinking about the *Rustler*.

Mr Pell said, 'Hang on for a bit, Sam. He won't find it easy to sell a boat in that condition. He may come back or something.'

I didn't want to spend every penny I had on the *Rustler*. She wanted a lot doing to her and it would take me years if I had to earn every penny before I could do her up.

But it turned out Mr Pell was right. Early one Saturday morning a beat-up old car drew up outside number sixty-four and there was a knock at the door. Mr Johnson was a man in his fifties, grey and haggard and dressed in a suit that had seen better days. 'Are you still interested in the *Rustler*?'

'Yes, I think so.'

He looked at me square. 'All right,' he said, 'I accept your offer—four thousand pounds.'

It passed through my head that I could beat him down another five hundred but something made me reject the idea. It would be wrong to buy the *Rustler* on a trick like that. Mr Johnson wanted the money right away—in cash.

'I'll get it on Monday,' I said. 'See you here at twelve o'clock.'

When I told Mr Pell, he said, 'You've done well, Sam—she's a good old boat.'

I persuaded the bank manager to give me the cash out of the deposit account on Monday morning and I had it in twenty-pound notes when Mr Johnson arrived. Between us we counted out the cash it had taken me twenty years to save. It seemed to be nothing—just four bundles of paper done up in elastic bands but I knew it was a load of sweat. He passed over the ship's papers to me and the Lloyd's certificate, signed me a receipt on a special form and the *Rustler* was mine.

'She's a good ship,' he said to me. 'I hope she'll do you well,' and then he looked at me with his haggard eyes, and said, 'You've got her for nothing you know.'

I felt sorry for him as he stuffed the notes into a battered briefcase—I wondered what urgent misfortune had brought him to this sorry parting with his boat. Then he went off and left me alone in the house, surrounded by pile upon pile of records. I never saw or heard of Mr Johnson again. Suddenly the loneliness left me like a bank of early morning mist, blown away by a cool, clean breeze—a breeze full of sweet anticipation and hope.

THREE

I wanted to move from Jubilee Street into the *Rustler* right away but I had to wait for Dick to come home from sea. We never knew when he was coming, he used to turn up every once in a while, stay for a few days and then be off again. As it happened he turned up within a month of Dad dying. He didn't seem in the least cut up about Dad.

He just said, 'You do what you like with the stuff, Sam. Anything you get for it is yours—you've earned it, looking after the old boy for all these years.'

We could do nothing about my sister. Neither of us knew her address and we couldn't find it among Dad's things. I only remember her from when I was a child. Mother told me she was ambitious, always wanted to get away from Jubilee Street and that Dad—and the music—had got on her nerves. She had gone soon after my other brother was killed. I showed Dick the *Rustler* but he didn't seem impressed.

'You're a rare bird, Sam,' is all he would say. 'I expect I'll see you about,' were his parting words. 'I'll drop aboard if ever I see the *Rustler* in port,' and then he was off.

I sold almost all the furniture for what I could get for it, which was precious little, and I persuaded a dealer in London to take the records.

Mr Pell said I could use the slip on a Saturday afternoon and Sunday. I got a couple of the lads in the yard to help me and we hauled the *Rustler* out. She was filthy with weed, but when we scraped her off we found her hull in fine condition. There was nothing to be done except to paint her with two coats of anti-fouling, repair the place Mr Pell had found in the stern and put her back again.

'You must've been born lucky,' Mr Pell said. 'You don't often see an old boat in that condition.'

The *Rustler* had been built down in the West country between the wars. She was pitch pine on oak timbers, she had a straight iron keel, and beautiful concave sections under her stern. She was broad and strong for'ard of amidships where the real bulk of her was and her bows faired away to a slim and elegant forefoot. Although she was sturdy and strong under the water there was nothing coarse about her lines. Whichever way you looked at her she was a beauty—a masterpiece created by generations of skill and experience handed down from one old shipwright to the next.

I took a week off work and gave the *Rustler* the biggest clean-out of her life. I went right through her from stem to stern, emptying muck out of the lockers, sorting her gear, throwing away junk and scrubbing her until she shone. I cleaned out the bilges and flushed them through with fresh water until they were sweet and I tidied all the junk off the deck, allowing the sun to filter into the cabin through the skylight. I found a treasure buried deep in the forepeak, a big ashtray turned out of solid brass in the shape of a ship's wheel with '*Rustler*—Falmouth—1932' carved round the edge. I polished it until it was like the sun. She was fitted out in teak and mahogany and the galley was handy enough when the layers of grease were cleaned off, and she had a small coke stove. Most of the fine woodwork had been painted over a dull brown, and she needed new settee covers, new pots and pans and crockery. She needed a thorough re-fit inside, but first she would have to be made habitable. The engine would run but it was temperamental and would have to be overhauled. I reckoned she would keep me busy on deck and below for the winter. I wouldn't sail her until the spring when I knew she would emerge from the yard with all her splendour restored to her. I gave notice to the council, handed over number sixty-four Jubilee Street and took up quarters on board with a sense of unbounded pride and a feeling that fortune had done me a favour. It was a bright October day when I moved on board and settled my modest belongings in their new home. In the evening I lit the cabin lamps, lit the stove and revelled in my surroundings. It was as if all my life had been slowly but surely working up to this climax of achievement. I was master in my own fine ship, with no debts, no ties, no responsibility except to myself and the seven seas were before me. I made myself a large supper, heaved a sigh of satisfaction and settled in front of my bogey stove with the newspaper, well enough contented with my new state of emancipation. The paper I had bought earlier in the day was *The Brighton Record*. I thumbed my way through it casually, my thoughts miles away from the petty scandals and irrelevant gossip. The Brighton Theatre had taken a half-page advertisement on a centre page. Julie Cranbrook in *The Masterpiece*.

I went the next night, which was Saturday. The play was a modern comedy of little consequence, I thought, but I wasn't concentrating so much on the play. I was looking at Julie and trying to summon up enough resolve to send a note to her after the performance. She was so sophisticated, so remote from the Julie I had known. There was an aged porter at the stage door. I gave him five bob and a piece of paper with 'Sam Pickson' written on it. He stumped off up a flight of stone steps and when he came back he said, 'She'll be down in ten minutes.'

I didn't know where I was going to take her—the pubs were just on closing. I got a real attack of nerves while I waited for her. What in Christ's name would I say to her? I was making a fool of myself.

She looked wonderful. She was wearing a pair of black slacks and a black sweater—no make-up, no brooches, no necklaces— just a mass of brown hair, brown eyes, a big smile and her tall, slim body. 'Sam, this is great. Let's go to my pub where we can talk in peace.' She hurried me across the road, down a side street to a small hotel. There was a tired waiter in a white coat. 'Evening, Miss. How was the show tonight?'

'Lousy,' Julie said. 'Two pints of bitter, Joe, please.'

For a minute I didn't know what to say. Julie was a bit overpowering. I wanted to ask her about Mr Cranbrook but I thought it would be better if it came from her, so I said, 'Julie, I've got a boat. Just bought her. She's at Newhaven—I'm living aboard. You'd like her.'

She dragged the whole story out of me, or rather she released some sort of catch inside me and it all poured out like the jackpot out of a one-armed bandit. I suppose I'd been longing to talk to someone about the *Rustler* for the past two weeks.

'Oh Sam,' she said. 'It all sounds wonderful, I haven't been on board a boat for years. Will you ask me on board?'

'Of course I will. When?'

'Tomorrow? I've got the day free. Can I come?'

Suddenly I got scared. The *Rustler* wasn't like the *Maydew*. She was smaller and ages older and she would be scruffy by Julie's standards.

'You mean just you?'

'Of course—no one knows anything about boats in this outfit.'

'She's in a bit of a mess, Julie, not fit for visitors really. Besides, I've no car. Only an old motorbike.'

'It's got a pillion seat, hasn't it?'

'Well, yes—I suppose so.'

I picked Julie up at ten the next morning from the hotel. I had been up since six, gave the boat a thorough tidy-up, swept the floor, cleaned the galley. As an afterthought I picked a bunch of blue sea lavender from the saltings and put them in a tumbler of water beside the brass ashtray on the cabin table. With the bogey stove going, the *Rustler*'s cabin was the snuggest place in the south of England.

Julie sat on the pillion with her arms clasped round my waist. As we drove over the downs towards Newhaven the pressure of her arms seemed to burn into me. I had the feeling I was going on a journey I would never come back from. It was high tide and the *Rustler* stood out over the saltings as she had the first day I saw her. Julie was silent as I rowed her out in the dinghy. She looked at the *Rustler* just as I had looked at her on that first day and then she said, 'Sam—she's lovely—she's a beauty.'

I made coffee and we settled in the saloon looking at each other across the table.

'Sam, she's nicer than the *Maydew*. I love her.'

We talked all morning, then I cooked lunch and we went right on talking all afternoon.

Consolidated Finance Limited had fallen with a big crash. Julie didn't know exactly how it had happened but there had been some financial jiggery-pokery on the part of one of the directors. Some irregularities had come to light, there had been a loss of confidence on the part of the biggest backers and shareholders and the company had been hastily wound up. The Cranbrooks' fortunes crashed with it, and they went from riches to comparative poverty within the space of a few weeks. Everything had to be sold to pay creditors: the *Maydew* went, the flat in London, the black car and the chauffeur, and Mr Cranbrook took the whole family to Australia where he still had some business interests. He had saved something, so they were not destitute.

At the time of their affluence Mr Cranbrook had settled a sum of money on Julie which she came into when she was twenty-one. She had come back from Australia by herself and had used the money on her training for the stage. Then she started her career in the theatre, which she had always wanted for herself. It wasn't easy and it wasn't much of a success. She did some television and radio work and occasionally she managed to get a season in some declining repertory theatre where she was underpaid, overworked, but happy.

'I hadn't got the right friends and I suppose I didn't want to go to bed with the right people,' she said ruefully.

She struggled for a few years, only just managing to keep her head above water and then she got married to the younger son of a lord. It was a disaster and didn't last more than a couple of years. Her grand in-laws despised her and were resentful because she had no money of her own. Her husband was a copy-writer in an advertising agency. He installed her in a nice flat in Chelsea and left her very much to herself, using her as a sort of housekeeper who could be relied on to arrange dinner parties for his friends. She found out quite soon that he was a practising homosexual. She had made one of the most fundamental mistakes a girl can make.

'The trouble is, I'm not sure that I'm really a brilliant actress,' Julie said, smiling wistfully. 'I love the theatre and I love the work, when I can get it. I may struggle to the top one day. I don't know how but one day my chance will come and I'll seize it. I don't really fit among stage people, Sam. I haven't much sympathy for the temperaments. They seem to act more off the stage than they do on it. I can't bear extroverts.'

By hard work and a really professional approach to her job, she had managed to keep going—just. She spent long periods out of work and she often took jobs that were so badly paid it was hardly worth doing them.

'To survive in the theatre you either have to have money or you have to be a bit of a whore.'

Julie was sometimes alarmingly frank. The Brighton job had been good, a three-month season at a reasonable salary. It was coming to an end soon and she had nothing else fixed although she had a chance of a job in Birmingham which might come off. I asked her about the boys. Robert had stayed in Australia and was doing well. He had a good job and was married with one child and another on the way. She didn't want to tell me about John, but I dragged it out of her. He had left Australia, against Mr Cranbrook's will, and had worked his passage to England. He had managed to get all sorts of jobs: in restaurants, at seaside towns in the summer, even on building sites. Sometimes she wouldn't see him for months and then he would turn up, usually when he was in trouble.

34

'The most awful thing has happened, Sam,' she said. 'He's got himself hooked on hard drugs—on heroin—it's terrible.'

I tried not to fall in love with Julie, but it didn't work. I somehow knew that no good could come of it—that if I allowed it to happen it would bring disaster. There was a chasm between us—class, education, upbringing, even temperament. She would always see things differently from me. She was imaginative, artistic, creative—I was, after all, a labourer on a building site. I had dug my education out of books for myself—Julie, it seemed to me, had culture moulded into her personality by inheritance and upbringing. Yet in the weeks that followed, we were inexorably drawn towards one another.

When I took her back to Brighton on that first Sunday night it was late. We had been talking all day.

She said, 'Sam, I loved today—it was wonderful. I think the *Rustler* is a peach. I hope you let me come again.'

I was in a turmoil of indecision the following week. My head was stuffed with Julie. I thought about her all day at the site and I thought about her all evening as I worked on board and I couldn't get her out of my head at night. I swore I would let the thing drop now, before it got too strong.

'Back out now, Sam,' I said to myself, 'while you still can.'

All the same, I found myself telephoning the hotel on Saturday morning. 'Julie, it's Sam—would you like to come again tomorrow?'

She was as beautiful on that Sunday morning as she had been on the previous one—she had tied a scarlet handkerchief round her head against the wind. On the road to Newhaven, she clung to me with electric arms.

We spent the day working on board, scraping the brown paint off the lovely teak and mahogany woodwork in the cabin. Julie had brought a piece of material with her and she made me two new cushion covers. She measured the saloon settees and said she would make new covers for these as well, if I would buy the material. It was late when we finished. It had been a lovely experience working together on the boat. Julie made me realize how lonely my life had been. We chatted away all day about boats and about her life and mine as well. I sensed that she was lonely too and was pleased to be with someone quite outside the circle of her acquaintances—the theatre people.

She said, 'Sam, why don't you take her out for a sail? See how she goes before the winter sets in?'

'I've thought about it, Julie but the gear's in a shocking state and the engine's not reliable. Besides, I'd like someone with me before I take her out for the first time.'

She said, 'The show ends next week. I'll come with you for a day, before I go back to London.'

I couldn't refuse her. When it was time to go back to Brighton, the bike wouldn't start—no amount of kicking and pushing would get a spark out of it and, of course, the garage near the yard was closed.

'You'll have to stay the night Julie,' I said, and we walked back across the quiet saltings to the *Rustler*.

I lent her a pair of pyjamas and made up a bed for her in the cabin. She looked magnificent in those pyjamas—red and white stripes. It was cosy in the *Rustler*'s cabin with the embers of the stove glowing red. I went to sleep in the saloon.

I got up early and pushed the bike up to the garage as soon as it opened. The rotor arm was worn and the engine fired at once when we put in a new one. Julie had breakfast ready by the time I got back and then I took her to Brighton and went late to work. The tides were just right for the next Sunday: high water in the morning and again in the evening. If it was fine there was no reason why we shouldn't take the *Rustler* to sea for a day. The weather had been settled for a week and the glass was high and steady. With Julie to help me, it would be easy.

I went to see the play the next Saturday night and afterwards there was a party on the stage to celebrate the end of the run— the next week they would all go off and look for other jobs. Julie was confident that her agent would find work for her within a couple of weeks. They were a strange lot, the theatre

36

people. They all called each other darling and seemed to speak in high-pitched, unnatural voices. I felt thoroughly out of place and left as soon as I reasonably could. I arranged to pick Julie up at eight the next morning. She was waiting for me in the hotel foyer when I arrived.

It was a perfect day for a sail. I had got everything ready on the Saturday. I told Mr Pell we were going to take the *Rustler* out and he said, 'You should be all right, Sam—the weather's settled—but I wouldn't go off too far if I were you—the state the gear is in.'

As soon as the tide was high we started. The engine fired first kick. Julie and I let go the moorings, the swing bridge opened and we motored out of the harbour. Julie was a natural: she knew instinctively what to do and did it without fuss. If anything, she was inclined to be a bit too quick—a bit impulsive perhaps, but she knew her way about the deck of a boat. She had the harbour ropes stowed, the fenders in, the loose gear off the deck and the halliards cleared away before we were through the harbour entrance. There was a good wind off shore and bright autumn sunshine with a few white clouds riding the breeze towards France. As soon as we were clear, I switched off the engine and we hoisted sail. The mains'l had a small tear in it near the clew, the stays'l had been badly patched, but the jib and the mizzen were good. As soon as she felt the wind the *Rustler* heeled gently and began to move.

I set a course out towards the Royal Sovereign. The great white bulk of Beachy Head was ablaze with the morning sunlight. The sea was a pale, cold green, the wind had a wintry edge to it.

The *Rustler* handled like a dinghy. She was faster than I had dared to hope. She was stiff and steady and she answered her helm it seemed, with an instinct of her own—like a sea bird wheels and sweeps across the sky. Julie and I hardly said a word —just big grins. I gave her the wheel and walked up the deck, looked over the bow as she sliced the waves, looked along the bowsprit and watched it snipping at the crests, flinging beads of spray into the wind, looked aloft at the graceful swelling of the mains'l, looked aft along the curve of her decks and astern at the champagne wake—looked at Julie standing square behind the wheel. This was the pay-off, the moment of truth. We put her through all her paces—brought her shaking and slatting into the wind, sent her careering off on a broad reach—ran her downwind on the edge of a jibe, hove her to, reefed her, goose-winged her mizzen on a run, allowed her to lie a-try. We measured her every whim and found her true on every count. 'Sam,' Julie said, 'she's wonderful.'

We sailed her out beyond the light vessel and then we hove-to and had lunch. The sea was quite rough now but *Rustler* lay as quiet and docile as if she were laid up in harbour.

Julie said, 'Sam, what are you going to do with her now you've got her?'

'Give her a re-fit. Make her into what she ought to be. What she deserves to be.'

'Yes, but after that, what are you going to do? Where are you going to take her?'

'I hadn't thought about that too much. I've been dreaming about her for years. I think I saw her a thousand times before she ever came into Mr Pell's yard. Now I've got her I can't quite believe it yet, it needs a different sort of thinking which I haven't got round to. I suppose I'm a bit slow that way.'

'You could go where you wanted, Sam: the West Indies, the South Seas. Even Australia if you wanted.'

I looked at her sharply, 'To see Mr Cranbrook, you mean?'

'Don't be such an ass, Sam. I wasn't thinking of Dad.'

We finished lunch and put her on the wind for a last thresh before going back. The wind had freshened now. She was pressed a bit under full sail, burying her lee rail and hitting the steep channel seas head on, sending spray high in the air so that the declining sun made a rainbow through the spume. It was wet and exhilarating. Julie looked pink and fresh and alert as we stood side by side in the cockpit. Suddenly, she shouted, 'Look out, Sam,' grabbed the wheel out of my hands and spun it so that *Rustler* luffed sharply. The next second there was a crack and the rope part of the weather runner broke, the bare ends flying through the blocks and the wire stay springing away and falling slack into the belly of the sail. The mast gave a sickening lurch, there was another crack as the rigging screw on the aft weather shroud stripped its thread. But already the strain was off.

Rustler came up into the wind complaining and shaking and dipping her bow into the sea. Julie and I never spoke. I left her at the wheel, nursing *Rustler* into the wind to keep the strain off the broken stays. I dipped the peak, lowered the jib and mizzen, tied two reefs into the mains'l. Then we squared off on the other tack, leaving the broken stay to hang uselessly to leeward and ran her off towards the harbour entrance.

'Sorry I pushed you off the wheel, Sam—I saw it stranding. I could see it was going to break.'

'Lucky we didn't lose the mast.'

We nursed her in without difficulty. It was blowing hard by the time we made the entrance. The engine wouldn't start so we edged her up to her berth under sail on the last of the flood tide and made fast. We spent an hour squaring up and stowing, then we had a meal and I took Julie back to Brighton. Some of the theatre people were standing on the pavement outside the hotel as we drew up.

'Look who's coming, darling. Whatever are you doing on that awful machine?'

One of the men, dressed in an army greatcoat, said, 'So that's what you've been getting up to on Sundays. All is revealed, darling. A peach on the pillion.'

Julie got off the bike and I said, 'Goodbye, Julie—hope you get fixed up with a job. I'll write to you.'

'Goodbye, Sam,' she said, and then softly to me so that the others wouldn't hear. 'I've loved every minute of it, Sam. Thanks a million.'

I let in the clutch and drove back to Newhaven, feeling like an old destitute tramp, waking to reality from a dream of unimagined beauty and fantasy. *Rustler* was warm and comforting but even she could not ease this new pain that seemed to grip me inside, clutching and twisting savagely at my heart. It was something new to me, a new and unexpected agony.

The agony went on. It didn't go away the next day or the next week or the next month. I went to work and absorbed myself in the boat as usual. I went through the day's routine like one of the machines at the site, labouring blindly and without purpose. In the end I came to understand that if I was to go on as before I would have to get things sorted out in my mind. I had always been a pretty contented and equable sort of character, I believe, taking life much as it came and going pretty much my own way, playing it by ear as you might say, and never letting things worry me. But now the world seemed to have turned round on me. I had reached a sort of climax and was unsure what to do next. I had achieved what I wanted after years of patient climbing and now I had come to a full stop. It was true what I had said to Julie—I hadn't really thought out where to go next. I had always assumed that the way would show itself to me naturally and without difficulty. Now, Julie had made it all seem impossible. I had tasted the freshness of her mind and now I couldn't do without it. I was hooked just as surely as John was hooked. In the end I wrote to her and sent the letter off to the Arts Theatre Club in London, 'Dear Julie, I'm sorry, I don't know how to put this very well, but what has happened is that I have fallen in love with you, although I swore I never would. I expect this sounds foolish—even stupid—to you because of the differences between us, but I would like you to marry me—get a divorce—and marry me. I had to write this letter because I've been so unhappy since you went away. I don't know whether you'll understand —I've been sort of confused and tormented. When I know your answer I think I'll be able to get myself sorted out one way or the other. I know you won't write me a long letter full of excuses. Just let me know one way or the other, love, Sam.'

I heard nothing for three days, then, one Saturday morning, I saw Mr Pell in the yard. 'Telegram's come for you, Sam, or something.'

I opened it very slowly, trying to keep calm. It said, 'Yes, love, Julie.'

Mr Pell looked at me and said, 'What's happened Sam? Come into a fortune, or something?'

I looked at him for a moment, and then said, 'Yes, Mr Pell, that's it. I've come into a fortune, or something.'

FOUR

Julie arrived the next day with a couple of suitcases. When I saw the taxi roll down the muddy track to the yard I went running across the saltings. We walked back to the *Rustler* hand in hand, leaving the cases in the yard.

When we were in the cabin Julie said, 'This is home Sam—my home.'

I kissed her for the first time in my life.

We lay for a long time, looking up at the deck-head in *Rustler*'s double cabin, following the parallel lines of the planking above our heads towards a boundless content—gazing out of the porthole across the soft, green wilderness of saltings.

She said, 'I've always loved you Sam, ever since I was a girl of sixteen. I fell for you all those years ago on the *Maydew*—fell absolutely, as girls do. The funny thing is I never really forgot. I always knew that somehow, somewhere we'd fetch up together. When I saw you in London—that night you were with your father—it all came back. I suppose you were a sort of romantic dream that I carried with me right through adolescence. I ought to have forgotten about you really, but somehow I never did. I thought I would see you again after that and when I didn't, I thought, "Oh well, I suppose he's married with five kids by now." Then when I saw you in Brighton you were just as I remembered you and when I came on board the *Rustler* it was suddenly for real. I felt I had come out into the fresh air for the first time in years. You didn't try to make love to me as soon as I was alone with you and you didn't lay on a lot of flattery and you didn't tell me smutty stories.

You treated me like a real person and it made me feel good. My world has been an unreal place since I left Dad and came to England, a place full of fake people doing fake things. Being married was fake. I was never in love. I was lonely and I wanted security. Instead, I found myself mixed up with a gang of perverts, which was bad luck I suppose. I walked out. It was the only thing I could do. I often thought of giving up the theatre but I love it really. It's what sometimes goes with it I can't stand but there's nothing else I can do. Sometimes it was rough— pretty near the breadline—sometimes it was rewarding. I got good jobs and the money was good when I was working, but I never knew how long it would be before the next job came along. Being without work was like ceasing to exist—all the emotion that ought to be coming out is bottled up inside until it chokes you. I shall never leave the theatre—I'm too tied up in it—always have been. It's just that to be able to interpret truthfully, I believe you have to live a genuine sort of life. You can't be superficial. Then she turned to me and her eyes filled with tears. 'John was another worry. Still is, if it comes to that. He seems to have a knack of turning up when I'm flush and I just have to help him out. I promised Father. He was in Brighton during the summer. He had some job in a garage and then he went on drugs again and they sacked him. For a time he lived on the beach with the rest of them, sleeping under the pier at night. Once or twice I had to cable father to send money. He always sent it, but really he's as broke as me. Then when I met you again all the old feelings I'd had when I was a girl came flooding back. I fell for you all over again.'

She clasped my hand and held it against her cheek. 'You're real Sam, you do real things. You've got a real boat. You've got it yourself by doing real work. The other people in my life have always seemed to me half fantasy. They don't work, they have jobs. They don't get things by their own sweat, they arrange things or get them from their parents. I wept when you left me outside the hotel that night, real tears. I thought I was going to lose you, thought I had misjudged everything and

43

that you didn't care. When your letter came, it was like some-one drawing the curtains and letting the sunlight into my mind.'

I had never understood what happiness meant until Julie came to the *Rustler*. She brought something quite new into my life. At first I found it hard to believe that she'd still be there when I came back from work. She soon got to know the people in the yard. Mr Pell thought the world of her, I could tell that. He remembered her from all those years back in the *Maydew*. He called her 'Missie'. She did the shopping and she did the cooking and she kept the *Rustler* like a new pin. She made new settee covers to match the new cushions, she reorganized the galley and she made the double cabin into a lovely place. She painted a little water colour of the *Rustler* lying in the saltings which we framed and hung in the saloon. We spent all our spare time through that winter working on the *Rustler*. After we had done the inside, we took the mast out, scraped it down to the bare wood, gave it five coats of varnish and put it back with new rigging, and that first half crown from the boat fund was set in the step under the heel of the mast. Then we renewed all the running gear and had a new suit of sails made for her, complete with tops'l and mizzen tops'l. We scraped the varnish off the cabin top, payed the decks and painted the top sides with three coats of pale blue and took off the flimsy doghouse. She was a real picture when it was all done. I stripped the engine down and overhauled it.

The weeks flew past that winter. Sometimes we would have a day off and go to London to a concert or to the theatre and sometimes we would spend the evenings in the pub talking and making plans.

Julie worked from time to time when the jobs came through. Her agent would send a telegram and she would telephone or go up to London to see him. She was a bit more choosy now about the sort of job she would take—now she would reject a season of repertory at Scarborough or York, but accept a tele-vision play or a couple of days' filming. I hated it when she went off. I always had the feeling she would never come back, but the money was good and I knew that it made her feel more independent.

The fund was slowly building up again in spite of all we spent on new gear, only now it wasn't called a boat fund, but a voyage fund. We spent hours discussing the great voyage. We decided to spend the summer in England doing short cruises, saving a bit more money, and testing the boat. At the end of the season, in September or October, we would go off—to Spain, the Canary Islands and then across to the West Indies. Julie had started the business of getting a divorce and we thought when she was free we might get married, and we might not. Julie was against it.

'Why get married?' she said. 'We trust each other, don't we? What business is it of anyone else whether we want to sleep together or not? Marriage is an admission of mutual mistrust.'

One day when Julie was in London working I had a visitor on board. I saw him walking towards the *Rustler* across the saltings. I couldn't place him but he was vaguely familiar.

'I'm looking for my sister, Julie Cranbrook,' he said. 'They told me she was on board here.' I knew at once that it was John.

'Come on board,' I said. 'Julie's in London. She'll be back this evening. I'm Sam Pickson.'

'Sam Pickson,' he said. 'That's funny—I knew a Pickson. Used to crew for my father.'

'That's right.'

'Good heavens,' he said. He came on board and looked round. 'Is Julie living on board here?' he asked.

'That's right.'

There was a bit of a pause. Neither of us knew quite what to say. I offered him a cup of tea and after a few minutes' studying me over the lip of the cup, he said, 'Are you the owner, Sam? Is this your boat?'

'That's right.'

'Good heavens,' he said. 'Is there ... well ... is there anyone else on board? ... or just the two of you?'

'Just Julie and I, John. We're living together.'

John looked uncomfortably round the cabin. 'She's a pretty old boat,' he said. 'Have you had her long?'

'Not long, John, just a few months.'

He looked pale, I thought, and not very well. He was much thinner than I remembered him. His lips were unusually red and his cheeks had a sallow look. His eyes were brown, like Julie's, but not calm and restful like hers. His always seemed agitated—always darting about, as if he was constantly on the lookout for some danger. He was ill at ease and confused. He asked me what I did—what sort of job I had. 'What are you doing these days, Sam?' were his precise words.

I thought for a moment and then I said, 'I work on a building site quite near here. I drive a bulldozer.'

'Good heavens,' he said. After a time he added, 'I'll just hop ashore, I think. One or two things to attend to—before the shops close. I'll come back a bit later. What time do you expect Julie?'

'About six. Sometimes she phones from the station and I go for her on the bike and sometimes she comes in a taxi.'

'Bike? Oh—motorcycle—I see.'

Julie came back at about half past six. I saw the taxi drive into the yard. I was always relieved when she came back—I hated her being away from me—always thought she might have some accident or not come back for some reason. I used to think about things when I was alone. I often had the feeling that in some way I had got something I wasn't really entitled to with Julie and that one day some figure of authority would come on board the *Rustler*, point his finger at me, and shout, 'Hey you, you can't have that—who the hell do you think you are?' and take Julie away.

'Hello, darling,' she said. 'It's lovely to be home again after that horrible, smoky city,' She kissed me and I put my arms round her and hugged her, as I alway did, to make sure she was really back.

'I've had a visitor—John. He's gone ashore, said he'd be back later.'

Julie sat down on the settee. 'Oh God, I suppose it had to come. How was he? Was he OK?'

'He was all right. I told him we were living together. He looked a bit put out.'

'John's an awful prude. I haven't got any illusions about him, Sam. It's just that I'm sorry for him and I feel responsible for him. He is my brother and, in spite of all his faults, I'm fond of him.'

John came back while we were having supper. He'd had a few drinks but not too much. I found him a beer and cooked him some supper while he talked to Julie. 'Couldn't think what had happened to you Julie,' he said in a rather aggrieved voice, 'you'd left your digs—simply packed up and gone without leaving a note or anything. In the end I went to see that agent chap of yours and he told me you were on board a yacht in Newhaven—so I came down to see what goes on—thought you might need some help. Then of course I met Sam here—remember him well—used to be our crew on the *Maydew*.' 'I ought to have left a note for you, I suppose,' she said, 'but I was so excited when I came down here—I didn't think of it.'

I could see that he wanted to talk to Julie without me being there but I wasn't quite sure whether Julie wanted to be alone with him or not.

'If you like, I'll go ashore to the pub,' I said to Julie. 'You two can come over later.'

John agreed at once but Julie said quickly, 'Don't do that Sam,' and then, turning to John, 'Sam and I are together you see—anything you want to say to me you can say to Sam—we've got no secrets.'

John climbed down at once. 'It was nothing really. What you do with your life's your own business, but I wondered whether

47

you've told Father about it. He might be a bit cut up you know ...'

'I'm going to tell Father next time I write,' Julie said. 'He always thought the world of Sam.'

John darted a look at me and then at Julie, and then he said, 'Listen, Julie, you are my kid sister, when all's said and done. I'd rather have said this to you alone but if you want Sam to be in on it—all right by me. Father may have thought the world of Sam as a crew on the *Maydew*—that's one thing. But whether he'll be pleased to hear that his only daughter is living with him on board a yacht in the mud off Newhaven—is quite another.'

'You mean living with the peasantry,' I said quietly.

I suppose I ought to have thrown him off the boat but I didn't because of Julie. Besides, you couldn't help admiring him for having the nerve to come out with it.

'You said it Sam, not me,' John said.

'No, it was you who said it first John. Way back on the *Maydew*. I don't suppose you remember.'

In an odd sort of way it seemed to clear the air, that conversation, and after it we talked amicably about all manner of things until it was quite late, although you could sense the strain in the atmosphere of the *Rustler*'s cabin. Julie told John about our plans to go off on a long cruise, down to Spain and maybe to the West Indies. She got out of John what he had been doing for the past three months. It didn't amount to much—he had been up north working as a salesman, had come back to London about a month back and didn't seem to be doing anything much at the moment. He asked Julie if he could stay the night.

'It seems to have got a bit late,' he said. 'I suppose I could get a bus to the station.'

Julie looked at me, asking with her eyes for an answer. I said, 'It's all right by me, Julie. It's up to you.'

She said, 'You'll have to sleep on the settee. I'll find you a couple of blankets.'

It was a strange experience, sleeping with Julie and knowing that someone else was the other side of a thin bulkhead, smouldering with jealousy and resentment. I didn't like it. I lay still and tense with Julie beside me, clasping her hand and listening to the noises of the night—the strange sucking noise as the falling tide drained off the saltings, the wild cry of a bird, the sigh of the cool wind through the rigging, the gentle crunch of the cooling and contracting coals in the stove, and at last the uneven breathing of our sleeping guest.

Julie turned her head and whispered quietly in my ear, 'It's all right Sam, I love you. Remember that. I love you.'

The feeling of strain was still there when we got up in the morning, although on the surface everything was amiable and calm. I made breakfast and laid it out on the cabin table: bacon and eggs, and hot coffee. I prided myself on *Rustler*'s coffee, thick and aromatic. It was splendid stuff to start the day on. I relit the cabin stove and a flush of friendly warmth spread through the boat. It was a bright January day and the early frost lay over the sheds in the yard and round the *Rustler*'s rail and hatches. I loved the winter. The air seemed to vibrate with crisp energy. I had been doing a job on deck, overhauling the anchor winch—like everything else on board it had been neglected and was seized solid with rust. Julie was busy painting out the bottom of a locker and John stayed below talking to her. I was glad they had the chance to be alone together for a bit. I didn't want John to think I was trying to drive a wedge between him and his sister. About mid-morning I went below to get a tool. Julie and John were sitting on either side of the cabin table and Julie was writing a cheque. 'John's in a bit of a fix,' she said. 'I'm lending him £50 to tide him over. You don't mind do you Sam?'

'It's nothing to do with me darling—it's your money—you earn it.'

'Just a temporary thing,' John explained, putting the cheque in his pocketbook, 'I'll let you have it back in a couple of weeks.' There was a bit of an awkward silence and then he said, 'I

49

must go Julie—got a train to catch—I'll drop you a line,' and he was off up through the hatch.

A few days later my brother Dick came on board. He got on well with Julie from the first moment—she was like her father, there wasn't an ounce of side in her. Dick was off for a couple of years—he had got a job on a tanker running between the Gulf and Australia. He had come to say goodbye.

We fitted the *Rustler* out in the spring and began to sail her. I took odd days off when Julie wasn't working and we would go for a voyage—down to Alderney, sometimes to the North Brittany coast, or the other way to Calais or Le Havre. We got to know the boat thoroughly, got used to handling her together and began to understand her and to know how hard she could be pressed and what were her limitations. The three of us, Julie and I and the *Rustler* became welded together in a sort of three-cornered partnership. Julie knew as much about sailing as I did myself and with her quick intelligence she often saw things first, as she had done the day we first took the *Rustler* out. Sometimes it seemed to us that the *Rustler* responded to our wishes with something more than inanimate obedience. She seemed to have an intuition and a will of her own. She was like a live animal. Little by little and without being aware of it, Julie and I had moved into a position of absolute well-being. Our world was an expanding one of happiness—too intense to be sustained, too far reaching for us to inhabit forever. I don't know where the streak of fatalism in me came from, but I believe I understood that this helter-skelter of rapture could not last—it was too good. Julie, I believe, took her happiness for granted and with few reservations. One summer night when we were sailing in the Channel under the blaze of stars, standing in the cockpit side by side and watching the *Rustler*'s endless games with the waves, she said, 'Sam, this is heaven—not up there, right here. You and the *Rustler*—everything. I love everything.'

Surprisingly, now that she wasn't forced to do any job that

came along, Julie got more work and better work than ever before. It may be that happiness suited her, that in some way she communicated to others the radiance of her new-found joy, persuading them by sheer force of her well-being to co-operate in her success.

'You might become famous, Julie. Are you sure you want to give it all up to come sailing?'

'Certain,' she said. 'I care about you more.'

She began to get small parts in television plays and films and then she would go off rehearsing for a week at a time. As the months passed and summer passed into autumn, we began to make final plans and *Rustler* began to look more and more like an ocean passage-maker. We got Mr Pell to make poles for twin running sails, and they were fixed in neat brackets one on either side of the coachroof. We bought an inflatable life-raft and made a stowage for it at the foot of the mast, and we had an extra water tank fitted under the after deck. We made endless lists of stores and bit by bit we brought them on board, stowing them away according to a plan we had drawn out in an old exercise book. Together we pondered over the spare gear we would need and made provision for its stowage. The *Rustler* began to fill up until she was like a ship-chandler and a grocer's shop combined.

'I reckon you're off into deep water, Missie, or something,' Mr Pell said to Julie.

We saw quite a lot of John. Once we took him sailing for a weekend. He led a strange life. He would work for a bit and get some money and then he would go into a prolonged drug session lasting, maybe weeks, until he got broke again. He was mixed up with a gang in Brighton and sometimes he would live rough, sleeping on the beach for weeks at a time. He seemed to believe that he was not hooked on heroin, that he was independent of its power and could take it up and put it down at will. He would regain some of his vitality, even put on weight between sessions and would convince Julie that he had given it up for good. Then he would seek her out, borrow money from her on any pretext and be off on another trip. John was Julie's real weakness. She didn't seem to be able to refuse him. He came to her time and time again and each time her cheque book would come out and she would give him money. I tried to stop it but I couldn't. She would agree with everything I said and the next time John came the same thing would happen. She knew that she was the only person in the world John could turn to, and she couldn't refuse him. It seemed to me that month by month he became more and more addicted.

The weekend he came sailing with us he was between trips and was pleasant enough. He was a fantastic swimmer and diver, graceful and strong in the water. It was lovely to watch him over the side, twisting and weaving with extraordinary grace. He could always get jobs as a swimming instructor or as a lifeguard, and he often worked at a holiday camp outside Brighton. He never dropped his air of contempt in his dealings with me but I didn't mind very much. He was really a pathetic character. His life was a sad progression from one degradation to another, from crisis to crisis. Julie helped him as much as she could and as far as I knew he never paid her anything back. His debt to her must have amounted to an enormous sum. He hated the idea of her going away.

'It's madness, Julie,' he would say, 'just when you're beginning to do well.'

He was frightened of being left alone. I think he began to hate me as well as to despise me because I was the instrument which would take Julie away from him.

We planned to leave towards the end of September. By then we reckoned we would have nearly seven hundred pounds in the fund. Julie hadn't managed to save much but she had helped with the expenses of fitting out and with day-to-day living. We never quarrelled or argued about money, we didn't regard it as anything of importance between us, we just spent what we needed to spend and saved as much as we could regardless of which of us had earned it. It was one of the nice things about our relationship. I reckoned the money would last us for a year, even if neither of us worked. We thought we might do a bit of chartering in the West Indies but, in any case, we planned to come back again after a year, earn some more money and decide what to do next.

Julie had a job booked in a television film in early September and after that, she told her agent, nothing more. She was to rehearse for a week in London and the film, as luck would have it, was to be shot in Brighton on September 15th. We planned to leave the day after, and sail direct to Spain. When Julie went off to London to rehearse, I gave up my job and sold the faithful motorbike. *Rustler* was as near perfect as we knew how to make her. We had spared no work or expense on her and there was nothing about her which had been neglected. She was full of stores, and her tanks were full. I squared up the bill with Mr Pell and by the time Julie came back on Saturday, the *Rustler* was ready. Julie and I walked all round her on deck and below, checking every piece of gear, looking in every locker, inspecting the engine, counting the stores, but she lacked for nothing. It seemed as if she knew she was going on a great voyage. After the months of preparation it was hard to accept the idea that everything was finished and ready.

'Another two days,' Julie said, 'and we'll be off across the ocean. I can't believe it, Sam—I suppose it'll be our honeymoon.'

FIVE

There was a telegram waiting for Julie in Mr Pell's office when we went ashore on Monday morning. Julie had arranged for me to go with her to Brighton to watch the film being made. It was from Julie's agent. 'Producer ill. Filming postponed until Friday.'

'Damn and blast,' Julie said. 'Just when we were all ready and set to go. What a damn nuisance.'

It was a nuisance. We had told Mr Pell and everyone in the yard that we were leaving on Tuesday morning. We were all ready and everything was carefully planned and now it would have to be changed. Mr Pell scratched his head when we told him.

'To tell you the truth, Sam, it puts me in a bit of a spot. There's another boat coming into your berth on Tuesday evening. She's a big 'un and I can't put her anywhere else. I suppose I could tell him not to come or something.'

'Don't do that,' I said. 'We'll shift into the outer harbour and lie alongside the quay. It's a bit uncomfortable but it won't matter for a week.'

'Well, it would help, Sam,' Mr Pell said, 'that is if Missie wouldn't mind going up and down the ladder or something.'

We shifted on Tuesday morning on the tide and berthed alongside the quay, ahead of one of the cross-channel steamers. It was a rotten berth compared to the familiar comfort of the yard. The ladder was covered in fuel oil and Julie got filthy when we went ashore to the pub that evening. There was wash from traffic in the harbour and the *Rustler* rolled and banged her beautiful blue topsides against the quay when a big tug went past in the night. It was noisy and smelly. At low tide we were down at the bottom of the world, dwarfed by the great bows of the cross-channel steamer, and the massive quay looming up alongside like the damp wall of a dungeon. At high tide the mooring ropes dipped in the water and saturated themselves with fuel oil. We both had a rotten night. The steamer went to sea, making a terrific noise and a swell which set the *Rustler* bashing herself against the harbour wall, the mooring ropes creaking and groaning. Loose dirt and gravel, kicked up by men working on the quay, fell like hailstones on the deck. While we were having breakfast on Wednesday morning a fishing boat tied outside us and the crew came stamping across the deck in heavy boots, climbed the ladder and when they came back brought more oil which they spread over *Rustler*'s white decks.

'This is dreadful, Sam,' Julie said. 'Can't we get out of here? Can't we go along to Shoreham? It's only a few miles along the coast and just as handy for me on Friday. I could get a taxi from Shoreham to Brighton just as easily as I could get one from here. At least we might get some peace in Shoreham.'

We were almost ready to go when John came along the quay.

'I thought you'd gone at first,' he shouted from the top of the ladder. 'The yard people told me you were out here.'

He turned his back on us to climb down the ladder.

'Can we take him along with us, Sam?' Julie said.

'All right,' I said reluctantly. 'If he wants to. That is, as far as Shoreham—but no further.'

She looked at me.

'I know, Sam. I know I've got to be tough about this and I swear I will be.'

'I thought at first you'd gone off,' John said to Julie. 'Gave me quite a turn when I saw the *Rustler* was gone. Thought for a moment I'd missed you—that you'd left for good,' and then turning to me, he said, 'morning, Sam.'

I found him an old pair of trousers and some rubber shoes and he helped us get the *Rustler* free of the fishing boat and the quay and into the middle of the harbour. I started the engine and we motored slowly out between the piers. There was a light breeze from the west—it was sunny and calm.

'It's only fifteen miles,' I said to Julie. 'We've plenty of time—if there isn't enough wind we can motor along in a few hours.'

John took the wheel. The engine was running smoothly enough but not as well as it should. It would cough now and again and a thin trail of blue smoke came from the exhaust. I knew what was wrong—the ignition was too far advanced. I had been meaning to fix it for weeks but it had always slipped my mind. Now was a good chance. We ran it for half an hour while we hoisted the sails and cleaned the oily mess from the decks and topsides. Then I stopped it, removed the wooden covers and took a small spanner to loosen the nut on the distributor shaft. The nut was stiff and wouldn't shift. Julie was in the fo'castle, right by the drawer where the tools were kept. 'Pass me the big spanner, darling—the shifter—the nut's seized. This one won't look at it.'

She opened the drawer, took out a heavy shifting spanner and came aft as far as the cabin table.

'Here you are, darling—catch,' and she threw the spanner across the saloon. She was always doing that sort of thing—I was used to it. She was impetuous, Julie was, could never wait to do a thing slowly. I tried to catch the spanner but it slipped through my fingers and fell into the engine. It fell on to the top of the distributor. There was a crack and the plastic cover split from side to side.

'That's torn it,' I said. 'I don't think I've got a spare.'

I tried to mend the distributor cover with glue and with tape and with wire but it was useless. I searched the locker where the engine spares were kept although I knew there was no spare distributor cap. It was just one of those things that had been overlooked.

'We could go back,' I said to Julie. 'We've got tide and the wind's fair. We'd probably get someone to tow us through the entrance if we needed it.'

'Let's go on,' Julie said. 'We've plenty of time and we'll soon fetch in when the tide turns.'

I decided to take a long leg off shore where the tide would be slacker and where we might find more breeze and then put about and fetch in towards Shoreham when the flood set in. We would probably be off Shoreham after dark, at low water, but we could wait at anchor if we had to and try to get someone to tow us in at daylight on Thursday if there wasn't enough wind. It was a pleasant afternoon's sail. We hoisted all our new gear—tops'ls, genoa fores'l and our biggest jib—and *Rustler* made about three knots on the off-shore tack. At about four in the afternoon when the tide was due to turn, we were already well abreast of Shoreham and about eight miles out to sea. We put about and began to fetch towards the land again. We could just see the chimney of the Shoreham power station against the hazy background of the low hills behind the town. Julie made us a meal and we left *Rustler* to steer herself and sat round the cabin table. John had been quiet and moody all day. He'd hardly said a word even to Julie— unlike him, he was usually cheerful and quite good company when he was with us on the boat.

'What's the matter, John?' Julie asked him. 'What's troubling you?'

'Oh, it's nothing, Julie. I'm doing all right really. I'm working at the holiday camp, have been for the past month. I just don't like the idea of you going off on this hare-brained trip, just when you're beginning to do well. It's crazy.'

'I want to go on this trip. Besides, Sam's being working for it for years, all his life practically. He's sweated his guts out for this moment.'

'OK, maybe he has. But you've got a career, a profession. Surely that's more important than beachcombing around in the sun. I don't know what's happened to you, Julie. You used to be so sensible, so stable. Now you've gone all to pieces.'

Julie said, 'I'm with Sam now, John. I told you that before. Where he goes I go. That's the way it is.'

Before sunset the wind fell away to nothing and the fog came down. It came swirling round us enveloping us in soft, moist floss. It shut out the sky and the sea, leaving us in a dim half-world. It threw back our voices like the walls of some sub-terranean chamber—it seemed to shrink the boat and to shrink us so that we became tiny people, living in an utterly reduced world. It was grey and wet and it penetrated every corner of the boat. Fat beads of moisture ran in rivulets down the sails and hung like pearls along the underside of the boom. There was a quiet which struck into our souls. The boat, the air around us, the sea itself were in a coma of inert moisture. Julie's warm breath condensed into tiny clouds which ascended into nothing like bubbles from a diver's helmet. *Rustler* was motionless, drifting on the tide in phantom circles, not answering her helm or responding to our wishes—lifeless as a dream in perpetual suspension. The fog induced in us a sensation of helpless apprehension. There was nothing we could do but wait and listen and wonder. John went to sleep in the fo'castle and Julie and I sat hand in hand in the cockpit, unwilling to break what seemed like a perpetual silence, contained within a watery mausoleum. When darkness came, the slowly twisting coils of fog drifted through a bowl of artificial yellow thrown up by the binnacle light, feeding the imagination with surrealist abstractions.

The damp began to penetrate our bones. We sat together for an hour, very close, our minds like our hands welded together by the damp and the cold.

Julie began to shiver gently. 'I'll light the stove, darling. We might as well be warm.'

The action was a relief. Soon the bogey was glowing red and the moisture dried out of the cabin. A thin line of smoke from the chimney rose vertically, pulling great mushrooms of fog upwards and out through the roof of our world. We stayed below, drinking tea, sitting on either side of the cabin table and listening for the occasional sounds that came to us from outside. From time to time the faint rumble of a ship's engine far to seaward and sometimes the stark cry of a gull, slicing through the silence with urgent alarm.

Julie said, 'If we don't get a breeze I'll miss the filming. Tomorrow's Thursday.'

'No need to worry yet. We've still got time and there may be a breeze with the daylight.'

But there was no breeze with the daylight and the fog persisted. Julie slept a bit, I sat in the warm, dry cabin listening, dozing off and then waking and listening again. The blackness of the night gave ground reluctantly before a dim and hesitant dawn. John and Julie got up and we made coffee.

'We'll have to tow her,' I said. 'I'll get the dinghy and we'll start.'

'Of course,' John said, 'splendid—we'll pull her along with the outboard.'

'We'll pull her along,' I said, 'but not with the outboard—we haven't got an outboard.'

'Good heavens,' John said.

I rowed first while Julie steered a compass course towards the shore. The dinghy was a small plastic pram. I braced my feet against the after thwart and pulled slowly and steadily for an hour. It took ten minutes to get the *Rustler* moving, but once she had gathered way, she came along easily. I could see her fore part looming up out of the sea behind the dinghy, could feel the rhythmic jerk of the tow line as the strain came on it with every stroke and by looking over the side I could see that we were moving—moving very slowly, perhaps a half or a quarter of a knot. I could hear the splash of the oars as the blades pulled through the water, the squeak of leather in the rowlocks and occasionally, a confused hum of conversation from Julie and John in the *Rustler*'s cockpit. I was reasonably fit and used to manual work, but soon my shoulders and my arms and back began to complain and the wooden thwart began to chafe. After an hour Julie's figure loomed out of the mist on *Rustler*'s fore deck.

'Have a break, Sam—let me have a turn—I've made some more coffee.'

'Get straight in the dinghy and keep her moving slowly and steadily,' I said as we changed places. 'Don't let her stop moving. It takes ten minutes to get her going again.'

John steered and I studied the chart and the tide table. It was hard to know exactly where we were. I reckoned we were seven, maybe nine, miles off shore. The tide would now be taking us west, but at eleven o'clock it would turn and we would be carried back towards Newhaven until evening. There was no telling exactly where we would come up with the coast and there was no radio beacon at Newhaven or at Shoreham to guide us. If the fog and the calm persisted we would just have to go on until we came into soundings and then decide what to do next. If the worst came to the worst and no breeze came, I could send Julie ashore in the dinghy and she could get a taxi to Brighton to be in time for the filming.

I came up into the cockpit where John was standing behind the wheel, drips of moisture hanging from the brim of his sou'wester and from the stubble round his chin. Julie, rowing in the dinghy could be heard but not seen. I glanced over the side and watched the water flowing past the hull painfully slowly.

John said nervously, 'I've been talking to Julie, Sam. I don't think she's dead keen on this trip—she's going because you're going, but she's not sure about leaving her work. Do you really think it's right? I mean to take her away like this—just when she's doing so well?'

'It's up to Julie. She'll do what she wants to do—you know that, John. It's not up to me and it's not up to you. She'll make up her own mind.' I looked at my watch, 'You give her a spell now, John.'

They changed over without a word. John took up the rowing

and Julie came aft to the cockpit. Her hands were already beginning to go red. 'Find a pair of gloves, Julie, before you do any
more. You can wear those smart ones you go to London in.'

'Will we get in, Sam?' she said. 'If I don't turn up they'll
have to cancel the take. It'll cost them thousands. I wouldn't be
popular.'

'We'll get you there, Julie. I may have to leave you on the
beach somewhere along the coast but you'll make it in time—
don't worry. We've still got the rest of today and all night.'

'John's been trying to persuade me not to go,' Julie said. 'He
says it's crazy—all the old arguments. I'm not giving an inch.'

'Listen, Julie,' I said. 'You've only got to say the word. If
you want to call it off, it's all right by me. We'll pack the idea
up. I won't take you away unless you're certain.'

'I am certain, Sam.'

John stuck the rowing for three quarters of an hour, then
he shouted, 'Julie, I'm getting tired. Is my time up yet?'

I went for'ard and he stopped rowing when he saw me. The
dinghy drifted alongside and he climbed aboard.

I settled down into the rhythm once more—this time Julie
had given me a cushion from the cabin to put over the thwart.
After a time the rhythm seemed to command my whole body
so that it worked like a machine which was separate from me
and not under my own control. I no longer dictated the move-
ments of my arms and my back and my shoulders or the stretch
of muscles in legs, neck and fingers—they reacted independ-
ently only registering protests by shafts of pain which darted
along my body like a random electric current. By moving my
position slightly I could ease one set of shocks at the expense
of others. By altering the set of my shoulders I could shift
the source of pain from one group of protesting mechanisms
to another. The fuel came from the rhythm. It had taken over
the task of converting energy into controlled movement. I
watched the dim shape of the *Rustler* astern of me growing
and shrinking in the revolving fog, and the jerking tow-line
lifting and stretching with each stroke and marking the water

with a line of droplets. I could hear again the muffled under-tone of the conversation between Julie and John. I wondered what new pressure was being applied.

Julie came to the foredeck when my hour was up but the rhythm was in me and I couldn't break it.

'I'll do another half hour,' I shouted.

She came back in twenty minutes. 'Please let me do a spell Sam—you'll break yourself.' I stopped rowing and climbed on board. Julie had the gloves on—they looked incongruous with her seaman's jersey and oilskin coat.

'There's coffee and a sandwich for you,' she said as she got into the dinghy.

John started in on me as soon as I came aft to the cockpit. 'Have you thought of the danger of it, Sam? After all, you're not really experienced at ocean sailing and anything can happen. Suppose one of you gets ill, or falls overboard, or has an accident? Anything could happen. You could be driven ashore or be run down by a steamer, or the boat could spring a leak or something could break. I know Dad won't have a minute's peace when you're out there by yourselves. He thinks the world of Julie—she means everything to him.'

I said, 'We know the risks, John. Julie understands perfectly. If she wants to cry off I'll cancel the cruise tomorrow. It's no use talking to me about it and I'd rather you packed up telling Julie these stories. It won't make her change her mind. You'd better go and do your spell in the dinghy. Take something to wrap round your hands,' and I tore a dishcloth in half and gave it to him. Julie came back and John took up the rowing for the best part of an hour.

'John's been working on me again,' she said. 'I know what it is really—he's scared of being left alone.'

I relieved John and kept on rowing. We kept on rowing all day, right through until the light went. Still there was no breath of wind, still the fog held us in a damp clasp, still we saw nothing and heard nothing. I knew we must be getting close to the shore—the soundings were down to five and a half fathoms but the shore along the south coast shelves steeply and I could see from the chart that we would be in deep water until we were no more than half a mile from the beach. At least there were no rocks or dangers off shore. I began to wonder whether all this effort was worth it—all for a couple of hours' film on the television. Julie hadn't told me much about the film but from the odd remarks she had let drop I gathered it was a trivial affair. If it had been anything worthwhile she would have talked to me about it during the rehearsals, given me the script to read and discussed her part with me. She took her work seriously. We would sometimes spend hours going over scripts. She would make me read her cues for her, and we would spend hours arguing about the plot and figuring out the interpretations she wanted. This one hadn't raised much interest. She only had a small part and when I asked her about it she said, 'There's nothing much to it, Sam. A good deal of sex, a bit of dirt, a few cheap gags and artificial situations, but it must cost thousands to put on and I don't want to be the one that lets them down.' All the same, I knew it wasn't the money that was making us sweat blood to get her there on time—it was Julie's sense of professional pride.

John's hands came up in blisters in the afternoon and I had to let him off rowing. Julie was tougher—she seemed to know how to conserve her strength and she had more determination and more endurance than John, which wasn't surprising. I kept her on half-hour stints because I knew that if she had to stop rowing—if she got too tired or her hands were blistered —I would not be able to keep going by myself without rests. John steered. It wasn't fair to expect either of them to do this work for long periods. I was used to manual work and my hands were hard as leather—John wasn't strong physically and he wasn't fit. He kept right on talking at Julie and me when we were not rowing. When it got dark I stopped and came on board, leaving the dinghy tied by the tow-line to the bow. Julie made us a meal and we lit the cabin stove again and sat round the table, too tired to talk.

John made coffee for us and then he pulled out his last trick. 'If you won't pack up the trip,' he said to Julie, 'take me with you. I can't manage by myself, Julie. I'll end up in prison.'

'In prison,' she said. 'What's the matter with you, John? Why prison?'

He was silent for a few minutes and then he said, slowly, 'Because I'm mixed up in something that will put me in prison sooner or later.'

Julie went all pale and her big brown eyes began to moisten. 'What do you mean?'

'All right, I'll tell you. You're forcing me to tell you. I can't manage, Julie—I just can't manage. I'm all right when I'm with you. I'd be all right here on the boat with you. I can get on all right without drugs as long as I'm with you or as long as I can get you when I need you. I've got no one else, you know that Julie. I swear to you I would never take drugs while I was here with you, but ashore, by myself, I have to have junk. I can manage on grass for a bit but every now and then I have to have some junk, and I have to steal to get the cash.'

'John, how can you say that? How do you steal? What do you steal? I don't understand.'

'I steal cars. It's part of a racket. I phone a chap in London I've never seen. His name's Charlie, that's all I know. He tells me what to get—a Cortina, a Viva, a Hillman—not more than two years old. He tells me where to leave it and I phone him when it's there. He sends me the cash three days later—fifty, sometimes seventy, quid. I've got door keys and ignition keys to fit anything,' and he pulled two bunches of keys from his pocket and threw them down on the cabin table. 'It can't go on much longer. I know it can't. Another chap who does it was picked up last week,' and then he turned to me, 'Sam, will you take me with you?'

I went out into the cockpit, leaving the two of them alone in the cabin. I didn't know what to say or what to think. To be in a small boat with John for months on end was unthinkable. It was something I would not do. Julie would have to decide whether to come with me and leave John to face whatever fate might have in store for him or whether to stay. If she stayed, the decision-making would be thrown back to me—whether to stay with her and abandon the voyage or whether to leave her and go by myself. John's power was stronger than I had believed. It was creeping into our lives and sowing the seeds of uncertainty and friction. The night was still, uncannily still as it had been the previous night, only the silent fog creeping round the boat and the plop, plop as drops of moisture fell from the boom on to the deck. Then I thought I heard a sound from somewhere ahead of us to the north. I went quickly to the foredeck and stood in the very bows of the boat listening with my hands clutching the forestay. It was music—the unmistakable sound of pop music being carried out to sea in undulating waves. I went back to the cockpit and took a bearing of the sound.

'Come on,' I said. 'I can hear the shore out ahead of us. I'm going to start rowing again—the course is 010°.'

I jumped into the dinghy and went back to the rhythm.

SIX

As I rowed, the music grew steadily louder—there was only one spot on the coast it could be coming from—there was nowhere else it could possibly be—Brighton Pier. It was now ten o'clock on Thursday night. Another hour would bring us close enough to drop the anchor. Then we could rest. All I wanted was to be still, all I could think of was an end to this interminable rhythm. We would have time in the morning to put Julie ashore in the dinghy, in good time for the filming. She was to meet the rest of the cast at the Metropole Hotel at eleven. I would have to talk to Julie about John—I didn't know what to make of it—I didn't know what Julie was thinking and I didn't know what John was saying to her right now in the *Rustler*'s cabin. Whatever it was, it was certain to be powerful stuff. Julie would be torn apart by doubts, but she would have to make the decision, I couldn't make it for her. I could only make my own decision and now I had no doubt about what it must be. I couldn't take John away on the trip—it would be disastrous. I couldn't go off for eight months with someone I despised, who looked down on me and probably hated me. I was sorry for John but at the same time I suppose I was afraid of him, that he would drive a wedge between me and Julie, that he would spoil our happiness, bring discord into our lives which, up to now, had never known it. In spite of my love for Julie, and hers for me, our relationship was full of hazard. As long as we were alone together everything was fine but I was afraid of people—people butting into our lives and exploiting the differ-

66

ences between us. John was more dangerous than anyone else because he was her brother and she loved him with all her capacity for compassion. The chances were she would call the trip off rather than leave John in the sort of trouble he was in. I rowed on, lost in the thoughts which were racing round my mind, oblivious to the pain in my shoulders and arms, unaware that the music behind me had suddenly become loud and clear.

Julie came running to the foredeck, 'Sam, stop rowing. Look, the fog's lifted.'

I turned on the thwart and saw that the lights of Brighton were spread out less than half a mile away. You could hear the hum of the town behind the music which came from the Palace Pier. The lights were a million fairy stars, twinkling yellow and green and red, doubling themselves in reflection from a shining black sea. Above, every fire in the heavens was alive with reflected brilliance and there was a great yellow moon high in the sky, throwing a flare path of silver across the sea. The *Rustler* was visible in every detail of her sails and rigging against the brilliance of the night. The gentlest of breezes, blowing off the shore, was ruffling her sails, the breeze that at last had come to blow away the fog. We were close alongside a small red buoy with a yellow flag—a racing buoy for the local sailing club, I assumed. I rowed a few more strokes until *Rustler* was twenty yards inside the buoy and in a line between it and the shore. It would serve as a good mark when the anchor was down, to check that she wasn't dragging. I climbed on board stiffly.

'Well done, darling, you made it,' Julie gave me a hug which drove away the stiffness and cold and the depressing damp.

I looked at the sounder which was showing ten feet. John and I cleared away the anchor and sent it over the side, the chain rattling merrily in the hawse. We let out fifteen fathoms of chain. Then we stowed the sails and hoisted a riding light. We had brought up between the West Pier and the Palace Pier, no more than a quarter of a mile off shore. It was just after midnight.

'You'll have to stay up, John,' I said. 'Keep awake and keep a lookout. Wake me if the wind changes or if you think she's dragging.' Julie and I got undressed and curled up together in the double cabin. Her body was warm and smooth and soft, an insulation against everything that was harsh or unpleasant or difficult. We both fell into a deep sleep.

The morning was fine and bright with the same gentle breeze from the north. The *Rustler* lay quietly to her anchor on a calm sea. The city of Brighton with its domes and spires and office blocks shimmered in the morning sunlight—the busy hum of traffic overlaid by the eternal music from the pier as if the city could not decide whether it existed for business or for pleasure. Julie and I left John on board and rowed ashore in the dinghy with Julie's suitcase and the broken pieces of the distributor cap. We left the dinghy on the shingle beach between the two piers, above the high-tide mark. There were only a few people about, an elderly gentleman walking his dog, a man picking up litter and a few children. I walked up to the Metropole with Julie. It was only a few yards along the Promenade and I left her in the foyer where the rest of the cast were already gathered.

As we walked along the front I said to her, 'Tell me the worst, Julie. Is the trip off? Or do we get away tomorrow as planned?'

'It's up to you, Sam. If you say so, we'll go—either with John or without him. But I wish we could get a minute to ourselves to talk about it.'

'We will, tonight, when you finish. If the weather's still fine we'll have a meal ashore and talk about it.'

Part of the film was to be shot in the hotel, part of it on the beach and part of it up on the downs behind Brighton. The producer was delighted with the weather and obviously relieved that all his cast had turned up. They would be finished by eight in the evening at the latest and I arranged to call for Julie at the hotel. If I didn't turn up she was to come down to the beach. If the *Rustler* wasn't there it would be because John and I had decided to move her, either to Shoreham or back to Newhaven. I knew that an anchorage off Brighton was risky. If the wind changed we would have to shift out of it at once. She couldn't be left alone there for a moment.

'I'll go into town and see if I can get a replacement for the distributor,' I said, 'and then I'll go back on board. But I'll shift out of it if the weather changes. If you don't see the riding light tonight, go back to the hotel and wait until I ring you.'

I found a good garage in the town with an electrical stores department, but the assistant shook his head when he saw the distributor cap.

'Haven't got that one,' he said. 'I'll ring our branch in Lewes and see if they've got one in stock.' He came back from the phone in a quarter of an hour. 'You're lucky, they've got it, but you'll have to go and get it yourself—this afternoon if you want it in a hurry—otherwise you'll have to wait till Monday. They're closed tomorrow.'

I went to the bus station and studied the timetable and then walked slowly back to the beach. I decided I would go to Lewes in the afternoon and get the distributor cap, if John would agree to stay on board *Rustler*. I could ask John to go, and stay on board myself, I supposed, but he was unreliable. Once he got ashore in Brighton he might never come back. I saw the *Rustler* as soon as I got to the seafront, lying as good as gold to her anchor, the red and yellow buoy immediately behind her. There was enough breeze now to lift her burgee and the sun still shone brightly. The beach was full of people now and a few were swimming. It was remarkably warm for late September. A motorboat with a cargo of trippers was leaving the end of the pier and she made a sweep round the *Rustler* before going off on her twenty-minute trip. I suppose a yacht lying at anchor off Brighton was something of a novelty. The music was blaring out from the pier, a sort of indiscriminate noise, non-music really. The dinghy was where I had left it but I saw at once that the rowlocks and one oar were missing.

I looked round, baffled, but the missing oar and the rowlocks were nowhere to be seen. I asked a lady in a red dress who was sitting on the shingle.

'There were some kids playing around it, duck, but they ran off just now,' she said.

I pulled the dinghy down the beach, through a mass of people who seemed to have materialized from nowhere and sculled out to the *Rustler*, using one oar over the stern. John had been asleep but he got up as soon as I came on board.

'Someone's pinched the rowlocks and one of the oars.'

'Good heavens,' he said. 'I'm not surprised—anything move-able goes off this beach within five minutes.'

'Of course,' I said, 'you know this beach quite well, don't you, John.'

I wished I hadn't said it at once.

'That's right,' he said. 'I know it well.'

I asked John if he was willing to stay on board and keep watch while I went to Lewes to get the distributor cap.

'There's a bus at two and another one back at half past three. I'll be back again by four at the latest.'

He agreed quite affably. The one o'clock weather forecast was fair. There was a 'high' over the Channel, the wind would be north to north-west, light becoming variable. Mist or fog expected in the night. There was a 'low' coming up from the Bay but it wasn't expected until the next day.

John said, 'You never answered my question, about me coming with you.'

I sat down opposite him on the cabin settee.

'I'm sorry, John, I haven't had a chance to talk to you since last night, and I haven't had a chance to talk to Julie either. I'm afraid the answer must be no as far as I'm concerned. It wouldn't work. I think you know it wouldn't work. To put it quite bluntly, you don't really like me very much. In a way I can see your point and I don't blame you. You don't think I'm good enough for Julie, and perhaps you're right. But we wouldn't fit as a threesome. I'm sorry but I just couldn't stand it. I'll talk to Julie about it tonight, as soon as I get a chance. If she's for it, I may think again, but it wouldn't be fair not to tell you what I think about it now.'

All he said was, 'Oh well, if that's the way it is ... I hope the trip goes well for you.'

John sculled me ashore in the dinghy and then took it back, so as not to leave it on the beach again.

'I'll shout when I get back and you can come for me. Thanks a lot.'

I remember feeling a bit uneasy about leaving the *Rustler*. I had a look at her from the Promenade and she seemed as peaceful and safe as a boat could be and precisely in the same position. I didn't see what harm she could come to in a couple of hours. The bus was a bit late starting, but I was in Lewes by twenty to three. The garage was outside the town on the main road. I found it in another quarter of an hour.

The chap looked at the broken distributor, 'This is a series "B", he said. 'The one we've got is an "A". It won't fit.'

He showed it to me. It was nearly half an inch bigger. He was a helpful chap and he phoned round to half a dozen garages. He located one in East Grinstead. By that time it was just on four o'clock.

'If it's really urgent,' he said, 'you could get a taxi there. You'll make it before they close at five.'

I went out and had a look at the sky. It was still sunny and there was no wind that I could detect. There was a low bank of cloud to the south, but that was nothing unusual for the time of year. I had to wait twenty minutes for the taxi.

When it came the driver said, 'Yes, we'll make it easily by five.'

I hated going off in the opposite direction to the *Rustler* but there was nothing for it. I supposed we could have gone off without the engine but it would have meant putting in somewhere else and wasting days, or going off to Spain without it, which would be unwise. We got to East Grinstead at ten to five. Within minutes I had the new distributor cap in my hand, the right model number and the right series. It wasn't so good going back. All the weekend traffic was pouring down the road to the coast. There was a solid line of cars belching fumes from their exhausts and proceeding at walking pace. There had been an accident somewhere along the road, the driver said, and there was single-line traffic at one point for nearly a mile and a huge build-up of cars. I longed for the faithful motorbike. Cars were a lunatic way of travelling. Outside Brighton there was another huge traffic block and it was just on seven o'clock when the taxi drove on to the sea front. I jumped out and looked over at the sea. The *Rustler* was still there. John had put up the riding light and you could see her outline in the light of the moon. I could even see a smudge of dark against the sea where the buoy was. I paid the taxi and walked briskly towards the Metropole. It was a bit early but Julie might be finished. She was just coming out as I arrived and I met her on the steps.

'Hello, darling, how did it go?'

'Fine.'

'Let's get aboard as quickly as we can. I've got the distributor cap.'

'Well done, darling, clever.'

We walked quickly along the Promenade hand in hand, down the steps on to the beach and crunched across the shingle to the water's edge.

'*Rustler* ahoy ... ahoy John ... come and get us.'

There was no answer. We stood shouting for half an hour but no reply came. In the dark it was impossible to see whether the dinghy was alongside or not, it might be made fast on the seaward side anyway.

Julie said, 'I can't believe he's not on board. Perhaps he's asleep, or maybe he can't hear us.'

The music was blaring out from the pier but *Rustler* was close enough. He ought to hear us easily.

'I'll have a look for the dinghy along the beach in case he's come ashore. You stay here and keep on shouting.'

I left her standing by the water and climbed up the beach to the wall of the Promenade where a few boats were pulled up. As I walked up the beach the black cloud that had been spread over the southern horizon since the afternoon, covered the moon and brought darkness. At the same time, I felt the first gust of wind from the south. Suddenly everything became urgent. Time was beginning to close in. I stumbled about in the dark for a quarter of an hour looking for the dinghy. The boats that were there were all heavy dinghies—too heavy for me to pull down the beach. None of them had oars. There was no one to be seen. I could hear Julie shouting vainly into the wind, which had already increased and a light rain had begun to fall. I ran back to her. We wasted another quarter of an hour shouting. With every minute that passed, the wind grew stronger.

'Julie, I'm going to swim out. There's nothing else for it. She might drag.'

I tore off my clothes and left them in a pile on the beach with the distributor cap. 'If John's there I'll send him ashore for you. If he isn't I'll sail her off. Wait at the Metropole.'

'Let me come with you, Sam.'

'You'd never make it, Julie, you know you wouldn't.'

She looked at the cold sea and the waves that had already began to break on the beach and said, 'You're right.'

I'm not a strong swimmer but I knew that, if I took it easy and kept calm, I'd make it. It was raining hard now and the wind had increased. All the same, there was no reason why the *Rustler* should drag her big fisherman anchor. It had held her in stronger winds than this a hundred times. It was a big anchor, on the heavy side for the boat, but I knew the bottom of a shingle beach makes rotten holding ground. I just felt a disquiet which I couldn't ignore. Perhaps everything was absolutely all right, John asleep maybe, *Rustler* holding secure to her anchor. This was the logical and sensible view. It was just that some mechanism inside me was working overtime, tapping out urgent messages which demanded attention. When you have a boat you develop a new sense, the sense a mother has for her child. A corner of your mind is reserved for her—thinking about her, worrying for her, heading off trouble for her. 'Keep calm and everything will be all right.' The wind was quite strong now and a squall of rain shut off the *Rustler*'s riding light. I looked back and took a quick bearing on two lights on the shore, one behind the other, to keep myself on course. I could still see Julie's trim figure standing on the beach. I began to get cold and the vicious little waves beat in my face making it difficult to see. Then the rain came down in a great torrent, shutting off the beach. It was black now, on all sides, and I began to be unsure of my direction. I could still hear the music off the Palace Pier. I kept it on my left side and struck on. The force of the rain beat down the waves making it easier to swim, but I was almost blinded by rain and then by hail which poured down like grapeshot, battering my head painfully and plopping into the water with a machine-gun noise. I struggled on.

What a bloody fool. What a blind, bloody idiot. If you want to lose your boat this is the way to do it. Leave her at anchor off Brighton beach of all bloody places. Leave her in the care of a bloody drug addict—for the sake of a bloody fool television film. Christ—I was getting tired, I could see nothing—only hear the zany music from the pier. I must be out past the *Rustler* by now. She'd drag ashore and be wrecked. I trod water, blinked through the blinding rain and turned to swim back before I drowned. Then I saw the *Rustler*, quite close to me towards the Palace Pier, dipping her bows into the short waves, snubbing at her chain. She was dragging slowly backwards towards the shore. I struck out with the last of my strength, hand over hand. I came up with her bows, seized the bobstay and paused. I wasn't sure I had the strength left to climb on board. I put my hand on the anchor chain. Every time she came up on a wave, I could feel the vibration as the anchor dragged across the bottom—maybe a foot at a time, maybe more. I reached up my right hand when she pitched, grasped the bowsprit shroud and pulled. The first time, my hand was dragged off the stay as her bow rose, the second time I hung on, got a leg over the bobstay, pulled myself up and climbed on board. There was no sign of the dinghy. I ran aft to the hatch and looked below. The oil lamp was burning, everything was neat and tidy but John wasn't there. I looked out astern. The hail had given way to rain. I could see the lights along the shore, I could see the black wall of the Promenade, I could hear the waves crunching against the beach. I switched on the echo-sounder—there was four foot of water under her. I would have to work fast, but if I used my intelligence I could do it. I reckoned I had ten minutes.

First I went for the tyers on the mains'l. The knots had swollen with the rain. I undid the first one, painfully slowly— not good enough. I ran to the companion—my knife must be there, hanging by its lanyard from a hook inside the cabin doors. There were two oilskins hanging on the top of it which I threw on the cabin floor to reveal the knife. I cut the tyers except the last one which tied the end of the gaff to the boom, and threw them aft into the cockpit. Then I cut free the jib in the same way, hooked it on to the bowsprit traveller and pulled it out, cleared away the halyard and clipped it to the head of the sail. The wind got under the sail and it began to flap wildly. I secured it with a slip-knot to the forestay, using a piece of the cut tyer and ran aft. I undid the mainsheet from its cleat, slacked off a fathom and made it fast again. I let free both highfield levers for the runners, then I spun the wheel to starboard, about half rudder. I glanced aft. The beach was close aboard and I could see Julie who was jumping up and down shouting something I couldn't hear. I had no more than two minutes left at the outside. I freed the last tyer on the mains'l, allowing the gaff to swing free, ran to the topping lift and pulled it up until the boom swung clear of the gallows. Then the halyards. I pulled the throat and the peak together. The sail seemed to creep up the mast slowly, slowly. When the throat was two blocks I made it fast and hoisted the peak, leaving the hauling parts in a heap on the deck. I slipped the tyer on the jib, ran to the halyard and pulled it up hand over hand, belayed it on its pin, raced aft to the port sheet and hove it tight. I was panting for breath and my heart was racing. The jib filled aback and *Rustler*'s bow payed off to starboard. For a horrible moment, she fell off towards the beach. She was suddenly broadside to it—Julie was jumping up and down in the rain, still shouting—I think she was hysterical. I thought I felt the *Rustler* touch bottom and then the mains'l filled and slowly, slowly as if the sea was thick black treacle, holding her back, she heeled to the wind and gathered way on the port tack.

I ran for'ard and heaved in on the anchor chain as it came slack. Then, when the strain came on it, I flung two turns round the bits, rushed back to the cockpit, spun the wheel and let fly the jib sheet. *Rustler* came shaking into the wind, hung there for a few horrible moments of uncertainty and then filled on the other tack. I trimmed the jib sheet, allowed her to gather way, steadied the helm and ran to the chain again. I saw the twenty-fathom mark come over the bow—it was unmistakable—twenty links of the chain were painted white and there was a piece of marline with two knots. John must have let out another five fathom of chain before he left her. I looked over my shoulder at the shore. It was further away. Julie was waving her arms and yelling her head off with joy in the pouring rain. I picked up another eight fathoms and then she snubbed the chain again and spun into the wind. She was a lady, this dear old boat—there was no tight spot she couldn't sail herself out of if you gave her the chance. The next time she sailed the anchor right out of the ground. I heaved the chain short and looked round. There was plenty of wind now. The rain had thinned and was being driven horizontally. She was sailing straight for the end of the West Pier—one more tack and she would be free. I put her about, noted that the light on the end of the Palace Pier was well off on the bow and checked the echo-sounder. There was fifteen feet of water. For the first time I realized I had no clothes on and was cold. I glanced round. There was nothing to be seen but the lights on the ends of the piers—the shore was already obliterated by the driving rain. She was clear—I went below. I found a sweater and a pair of trousers and for good measure a stiff tot of brandy out of the locker over Julie's bunk. In ten more minutes she'd be away to sea and I would be able to take stock and decide where to go.

SEVEN

I was never a person to believe much in luck, particularly where boats are concerned. You get from the sea pretty much what you deserve. Most of the bad luck people complain about is nothing more than mismanagement, lack of concentration, lack of vigilance or a failure to think ahead and to take account of every circumstance. The sea doesn't suffer fools gladly— in the end they usually pay for their errors and indiscretions. What happened to the *Rustler* was bad luck in the sense that it might easily not have happened, but I could never lay the blame for it on anything or any person but myself—least of all the *Rustler*. I made the facile mistake, an unpardonable one, of thinking the battle was won before it was over. I don't believe I'll ever make that mistake again—I paid a hard price for the lesson.

While I was putting on a pair of trousers I heard a metallic bang on the port side of the hull for'ard, and then a series of smaller bangs along the topsides and a scraping noise under the boat. I knew at once what it was—the buoy. We had run foul of the buoy with the little yellow flag. I was out in the cockpit in time to see it on the lee side, pressed under the sea by the *Rustler*'s keel, laid over on its side, the flag just breaking water. I watched it, fascinated, with a lump in my throat and a cold feeling in the centre of my spine, wondering if it would pass clear of the hull. It didn't. The buoy's mooring chain slipped into the crack between the rudder and the sternpost and the *Rustler* brought up all standing, pinned by her tail.

At once her head payed off towards the shore. For a moment I simply stood in the cockpit, dazed by this twist of fortune. *Rustler* hung for a minute, heeling over to port, the sails and sheets straining, the bowsprit describing an arc to landward until it was pointing directly at the beach. Then the chain broke somewhere near the bottom and she set off for the shore like a greyhound out of a trap. I tried to move the wheel but the rudder was jammed solid. I ran for'ard and threw off the peak and throat halyards. The peak dropped down but the throat was jammed by the force of the wind. I glanced over the side—the water was racing past—she must be doing seven knots, the buoy with its yellow flag, towing behind like a surf rider. I let go the jib halyard and the sail went off, streaming out ahead, flapping and shaking. I let go the anchor chain. It ran out with such force that sparks flew up from the hawse. It was impossible to touch it. It ran out until it fetched up against the shackle in the locker with a bang like a cannon shot, but nothing stopped the *Rustler*—she careered on, drunk, out of her mind, wild with uncontrollable destructive force. I knew that nothing I could do could have the slightest influence on her now—she was beyond the control of any hand. So obedient, so tractable, so good-natured and obliging, she had suddenly turned about, had taken life between her jaws and with a snarl of fury had summoned her strength for a headlong leap to destruction. I saw the beach coming and braced myself against the shrouds. She hit full tilt. The masts shook, the rigging jerked taut. I heard things in the cabin leave their moorings and tumble towards the bows. Then she gybed sickeningly, her stern slewed round and she came to rest, broadside on to the beach. It had all happened in minutes—she had turned herself into something different. From being a part of the sea, a creature tuned to her element, with a shrewd intelligence of her own, she had become an inert bundle of wood, copper, iron and lead—a part of Brighton beach with the waves breaking against her side and flinging spray over her decks.

I took down the mains'l, hauled the boom down on the gallows and tied the sail up with a piece of rope. I remember that I went about the jobs that had to be done mechanically, without being fully aware of what had happened. The *Rustler* was almost upright, held by the slope of the beach. The waves banged against the portside, causing her to shudder and tremble. Sometimes a larger one would hit her amidships and send a column of spray leaping into the rigging. I pulled the jib in over the bow, folded it loosely and stowed it in the fo'castle, took down the riding light which was still burning, coiled down the halyards and cleared up some of the cut ends of the sail tyers which were lying untidily about the deck. Then I went below. The bookcase had been wrenched off its fastenings by the force of *Rustler*'s impact with the beach, and books were strewn over the cabin. The galley was a shambles. Pot and pans had come off their hooks, plates had jumped out of their stowage and broken china lay over the cabin floor, the kettle had up-ended itself, emptying its contents into an open tin of biscuits. The washing-up mop had taken up a new position head down in a jar of treacle that had mysteriously lost its lid. The cabin gave the appearance of studied and purposeful chaos, as if some person had set out to overturn the natural order of life and to create a situation of confusion and revolt. Julie's black beret was inexplicably hanging from one of the skylight fittings. I took it down, looked at it and wondered what had happened to her. She must have gone back to the hotel as soon as the *Rustler* got clear, running along the promenade as fast as she could, to get warm and dry. She would have been spared the humiliation of seeing my final degradation—*Rustler* would have been out of her sight in the driving rain. I thought of going to the hotel but decided not to. It would be kinder to let her sleep a night in the happy belief that everything was well. I found some tea and a tin of condensed milk, made myself a hot drink and sat on the starboard settee in my wet clothes, listening to the thunder of the seas and feeling the *Rustler* shake with the impact of each new wave as if I myself were experiencing her torture.

I must have slept until morning. I was so stiff and cold when I woke that I could hardly move. It was Julie's voice that woke me.

'Sam, Sam, where are you, Sam?'

It was like a voice coming out of a long tunnel, bouncing from side to side and swelling in volume. I heard her climb up the bobstay to the deck and the next moment she was in the companionway, still dressed in her smart clothes, her hair hanging over her face, her expression all concern and anxiety.

'Sam, darling, are you all right?'

She was beside me, sobbing in my lap.

'Oh, Sam, I thought something terrible had happened to you. I thought you were drowned, or hurt, or something horrible. Are you all right really? Tell me you're all right, Sam.'

'Yes, I'm all right, Julie. The poor old boat's done for but I'm all right.'

I rehearsed to her the whole macabre business in retrospect.

'I kept shouting to you to watch out for the buoy but you didn't hear me. Then you got off so wonderfully I thought everything was all right and I went back to the hotel. When I woke up this morning I looked out of the window and I couldn't believe it. I was petrified. I thought something horrible had happened, or you would have come up to the hotel. Oh, Sam, I'm so glad you're safe. Nothing else matters, except you.'

She made me put on some dry clothes and she lit the stove. She created order out of the mess in minutes, made coffee and gave me some breakfast.

'Don't worry about the *Rustler*, Sam. We'll get her off. We'll fix her up if she's damaged and we'll get her off on the next tide. It doesn't matter if we have to put the trip off till next year, Sam. Everything will be all right, as long as you're all right.'

She coaxed back my confidence like a magician.

I went out and looked round me. It had stopped raining but it was blowing harder than ever—the wind was whistling and whining through the rigging. It was low tide now and the sea was twenty yards away. Big waves had built up and were rolling in and hurling themselves on the beach in a smother of white. The beach was quite flat but it rose sharply in a bank of shingle where the *Rustler* lay, near the high-tide mark. The buoy was lying astern, twenty feet of chain stretching out towards the sea. The *Rustler*'s anchor chain was stretched down the beach from the bow, disappearing into the water. I jumped down on to the shingle and walked round the boat. Nothing could be seen of the starboard side, because it lay up against the shingle bank, but the portside seemed to be undamaged except for some scraped paint round the turn of the bilge where the buoy chain had fouled her. I cleared the chain from under the rudder and it came away ludicrously easily. I went down to the edge of the sea and pulled at the anchor chain. To my surprise it came in quite easily. When the anchor appeared out of the water I saw the chain was half-hitched round one of the flukes. No wonder she had dragged. It was hard to understand how it had happened. I knew the anchor was clear when I let it go and I had dropped it carefully, I had felt it bite into the bottom, before I had allowed the chain to run out. It couldn't have been more foul if somebody had done it on purpose. Then I climbed back on board and looked at the tide table in the almanac.

'We've bought it, Julie,' I said. 'Last night's tide and today's are the highest spring tides of the year. After today they begin to take off. If we don't get her off today, we'll be in dead trouble.'

Julie didn't say anything about the tides. I thought maybe she hadn't taken it in about the springs. It meant that after this high tide, there wouldn't be another one as high at least until next year.

She said, 'What's happened to John? Have you seen him?'

'Disappeared—gone off with our dinghy—what on earth's happened to him?'

'He hasn't gone with the dinghy,' Julie said. 'It's on the beach.'

She pointed it out to me, lying up against the Promenade.

It still had one oar in it, you could see the blade sticking out over the stern.

'I saw it this morning when I came on board.'

'That's funny,' I said. 'I could swear I looked there last night.'

'It was pitch dark, darling. You might have missed it.'

'Well, yes. I suppose I might have.'

'It all seems so long ago,' Julie said. 'I'd almost forgotten about John. He was very depressed when I was talking to him, while you were rowing. I told him there wasn't a chance of you letting him come with us and anyhow, I told him I didn't want him to come either. I explained to him that it was our trip, our thing and we couldn't possibly take anyone else. He went all pathetic—said he didn't know what would happen to him—said he'd end up in prison. I gave him some more money, made him promise never to steal again and he did promise. I gave him all the money I had in the bank and some more besides. I'll be overdrawn until my cheque comes from yesterday's filming. That'll just cover it. Are you angry with me, Sam?'

'I'm not angry, it's your money. You can do what you think you ought to do, but it's a pity. We might need all the money we've got before this lot's over.'

I told her about the conversation I had had with John, while she was filming.

'I told him the same. I told him that if you really wanted him to come I might think about it again.'

'It wouldn't work, Sam,' she said. 'I know it wouldn't work. I just want to be with you, away from all this, away from films, people, everything. But I'd like to know what's happened to John now. I'd like to know why he went off like that.'

'If he's got some money,' I said, 'I expect he's gone off on a trip.'

I started work at once. There were some people about now. There was a line of spectators standing along the top of the Promenade, all dressed up in coats and scarves and mackintoshes against the wind and the occasional driving rain. There were a dozen more standing on the shingle by the *Rustler*. I knew it was going to blow harder when the tide came up. I was scared for the *Rustler*. When the waves came up the beach at high tide, driven by a hard southerly gale, they would give her a terrible pounding. The barometer was way down and still falling.

'Can't we get some help?' Julie said. 'There must be someone among all these people who'd be useful.'

'I doubt it. I wouldn't mind having someone with a bit of knowledge, but I doubt whether any of these chaps would be much help.'

'Why not try Mr Pell? He could send someone over from the yard. They'd be here inside an hour.'

'It's Saturday. There won't be anyone there and Mr Pell's not on the phone at home, but it's an idea. Go and telephone. See if you can raise anyone. I'll start laying out the anchor.'

She went off to phone and I started dragging chain down the beach.

'Anyone like to give a hand?' I asked the people on the beach. There were about twenty of them now, standing in a knot out of the wind in the *Rustler*'s lee. They shifted their feet a bit.

A large man said, 'I'd like to, but I've got to go off and meet my wife in a few minutes.'

'Well, if you can't help, I'd be obliged if you'd mind clearing off and leaving us to get on with it.'

A few went off but the rest, sensing an impending disaster, lingered on, clinging like ghouls to their positions in the front row of the stalls. I pulled a pile of the anchor chain down the shore to the water's edge, then I got another anchor out of the *Rustler*'s after peak, made a bridle with a spare piece of chain and shackled it all together about twenty feet from the end so that I had two anchors spread out from the same chain. I made fast a length of rope to the end of the spare chain with a fender tied to it. As soon as *Rustler* was afloat and over the bridle, I would slip the shackle, let the spare anchor go and come back for it another time. The tide was already beginning to make. I hadn't much time. When I got back, Julie came running across the shingle from the Promenade, pushed through the spectators and came on board.

'I wish these people would go,' she said. 'I can't get any reply from the yard, Sam. The phone just rang and rang.'

'Don't worry, darling, we'll do it ourselves.'

But I didn't feel as confident as I sounded. All hell would be let loose on that beach at high tide. I changing into swimming trunks. People were peering into the cabin through the port-holes, jostling for position.

'Going in for a dip, mister?' a youth said as I came out of the cabin, a girl giggled and they all looked at each other and smiled. It was a good Saturday morning's jaunt.

I carried the anchors into the water and as far out as I could get them. The sea was rough now, and it wasn't easy but I got them both firmly settled into the shingle in a 'V' from the shackle, making certain that neither of them was foul. They didn't look as though they could drag. We were lucky the *Rustler* had her starboard side to the shore. The roller for the anchor chain was a stout fitting, bolted to the stem on the port side giving the chain a clear lead away from the boat. If she had been the other way round, the chain would have led round the bow and under the bobstay. It would have fouled when the strain came on it. *Rustler*'s winch was a hefty affair, with two gears, which could lift a tremendous weight. I dragged the slack back on board and turned the winch until chain was lying in a straight line down to the water's edge. I picked up the buoy with the yellow flag and dragged it up the beach out of the way, making the chain fast to a post for good measure. If only the wind would give us a break it might not be too difficult to get her off. I was cold as I made my way through the spectators and came back on board. By this time there must have been a couple of hundred of them, including those on the Promenade. Julie gave me a steaming cup of coffee and rubbed me with a towel. She gave me the spare distributor cap for the engine which she had brought from the beach the previous night. We stripped the plug leads from the old one,

85

fitted them and clipped it into place. I touched the starter button and the engine roared into life. We ran it for a moment and then switched off. It would soon run hot without circulating water. I glanced at her. She had the broken pieces of the old cap in her hands, her eyes were full of tears.

'Don't be an ass, Julie. It was just one of those things. Don't worry about whose fault it was. That won't make any difference now. All we've got to do is get her off.' I gave her a quick kiss. 'Come on, we'll get the sails reefed.'

We tied three reefs in the mains'l, working slowly and methodically and doublechecking that every point was tied properly and that the sail was free to run up clear. We got a small jib out of the locker, bent it on so that it was ready for hoisting and tied it securely down so that the wind couldn't get under it. It was blowing a real gale now. The waves were beating against the shore, the tide was coming up fast, the wind was heavy, tearing at the furled sails and making it difficult to stand on deck. I thought hard but there was nothing more we could do to prepare the *Rustler*, only wait for the tide to come up.

Julie and I sat in the cabin, silent and dispirited. You could feel the *Rustler* tremble in the gusts, shaking herself right through to the keel so that plates and glasses on the cabin table vibrated gently. She was shuddering as if in fear of what was to come to her in two hours when the tide was high and the seething water was round her.

'Are we going to make it, Sam?' Julie asked.

'We may, but we shall need some luck. As soon as she begins to lift, I'll start taking in chain, a foot at a time, as I can get it. Her bow will swing off and her stern will begin to pound. Whether she'll start a plank or damage the stern post or the rudder, is anyone's guess. As soon as the bow's far enough off, I'll give you a wave. Slam her full ahead and I'll engage high gear and wind like hell. Then put the helm to port and we'll wind up as far as the bridle. She'll have a good six feet under her there at high tide. Then we'll decide what to do—hold on for a tide and let the weather ease or sail her off with the engine running. We'll probably sail her off—I don't want to risk pounding her to pieces when the tide begins to go down.'

Already the waves were lifting her under the turn of the bilge, slapping up under her with a hollow sound, punching her in the belly. Julie and I put on oilskin suits and went out into the cockpit. Spray was lashing across her now and the spectators had fled from the beach. It was hard to hear yourself speak over the shriek of the wind. Ahead of us, the waves were crashing against the West Pier. At times they would break right over the end of it, the water cascading back into the sea in a hundred angry white waterfalls. The sky was a thick blanket of grey and close down over the breakers, wisps of blacker cloud came racing in off the ocean. To seaward, a wilderness of breaking waves, wild, confused masses of water spending their pent-up energy in a show of violent destructive force, were slowly and with relentless purpose converging on the *Rustler* as the tide rose. They would break on the beach and send their crests hurtling against the topsides as if the *Rustler* were some enemy that they were dedicated to destroy. She shuddered and shook with each new impact.

As the minutes dragged on, the fury of the wind seemed to gain force with the rising tide. Now the *Rustler* was lifted a fraction clear of the bottom by each wave and allowed to fall back with a sickening jolt. The masts and rigging shook, the pounding seemed to go right through her, to shudder through every timber and every fastening. Her whole frame set up an urgent complaint against a cruel and senseless punishment. I looked in at the cabin clock—it was a quarter of an hour to high water. Julie and I stood in the cockpit, lashed by stinging spray, grasping the coamings for support, watching and waiting while the sea came hungrily round the *Rustler*, feeling round her body with greedy fingers, grinding her into the abrasive shingle, shaking her so that she jarred and shivered with each new impact.

I nodded to Julie and shouted at her through the commotion, 'Get the engine going—I'll start.'

As I made my way for'ard along the weather side of the deck, moving cautiously from handhold to handhold, a wave hit amidships. It sent a column of spray up to the cross-trees and solid water poured aboard, gripping my body and streaming it to leeward as I clung for my life to the shrouds. Seconds later, another hit aft. I glanced at Julie. She hung to the mizzen rigging as the cockpit filled with water. She looked at me when it passed and smiled. Her sou'wester had gone and her hair streamed in the wind. I could hear the engine ticking over. *Rustler* was lifting on the combers now, rearing up and hurling herself down on the shingle with a force that must break her soon. I grabbed the winch handle and began to turn. Link by link the chain began to come in. I looked over the trembling end of the bowsprit and took a mark against the inner part of the West Pier. At first, she didn't move. The anchors must be dragging. I turned on, it seemed for an age, feeling the *Rustler's* agony under me, cringing inside myself as she struggled through her pain. Then the bowsprit began to move along the pier. Suddenly the strain on the chain eased. I slammed the winch into high gear and turned the handle with all my strength—now the chain was coming in fast.

I shouted to Julie standing at the wheel up to her waist in water, 'Put her ahead,' I shouted and waved my arm. Immediately I felt the throb of the engine.

The *Rustler* began to move. As her bow slowly swung to seaward she came upright and we felt her sternpost grind into the gravel. The next wave lifted her high in the air as a mountain of boiling water slid underneath her. She hung for a terrifying instant as if suspended in a cloud of foam. I turned the winch wildly, the propeller was roaring and vibrating—this must be her last fall. But now there was more water under her. She banged but now she had an imperceptible cushion of water to ease her fall. I looked aft.

Julie was jumping up and down in the cockpit and shouting, 'She's coming Sam, she's coming.'

It was true, she was coming. She was moving ahead, scraping and grinding into the gravel, still at an angle to the line of her anchor chain, but she was coming. As I wound the winch she kept on coming, her bow turning towards freedom and the open sea. Every reserve of energy I possessed went into the winch. I turned it to the exclusion of any other thought, I concentrated all the power at my disposal on the winch. I could see only the chain creeping in over the roller, link by link, foot by foot, yard by stubborn yard. The banging and the jolting and the grinding ceased. The beach at Brighton seemed to have been cheated of its victim as the *Rustler* moved into deeper water.

She might have come off. She ought to have come off. We had done everything as it should be done and we had a right to be rewarded. But some perverse quirk of the divine ordinance decreed otherwise. A wave bigger by far than its fellows, a giant, marching across the green fields of the ocean with the accumulated momentum and dignity of the deep contained within it, a freak thrown up by the unpredictable mathematics of the sea, struck the *Rustler* square on her forepart at the turn of the bow, for'ard of the chain plates. I saw it coming, saw it rear up above me, its concave face turning in on itself. I gazed for a moment into the very eye of this unstable wall of swaying water, already toppling towards me, the heavy white crest poised and ready to spring. And then it burst apart, released its energy in a last expression of sullen vindictiveness. I let go the winch handle and threw my arms round the bitts. A second later, tons of water descended over me from above, enveloping me in a pale green shroud of water, flattening me to the deck, pulling at my arms so that I thought the force would tear them from their sockets. I saw out of the corner of my eye the chain roller wrenched out of the stem and bent sideways like plasticine. The chain jumped clear of its constraint, tore away the stanchions and the bulwarks along the port side as if they were made of some inconsiderable material, jumped off the winch like a whipcord and ran out of the hawse with a roar of fury. The *Rustler*'s bow payed off and for the second time that day she drove helter-skelter up the beach at Brighton.

EIGHT

She ran aground as she had done before, slewing herself round
so that her port side was to seaward. This time the wind was
fiercer and the waves were three times as big and powerful.
The first one that caught her under her bilge lifted her bodily
and moved her sideways up the shingle. Now she lay on her
side, the whole of her flank exposed and vulnerable. With each
new battering she edged herself sideways up the beach, like
an animal cringing from a cruel assault. The punishment went
on, each big surf pushing her inch by inch up the beach until
the tide was high. She was now above the normal high-water
mark, at the top of the beach, not so far from the Promenade
itself, where, in moderate times, the sea never reaches. Now
she was over the top of the bank of shingle she had rested
against when she first grounded.

I was still lying on the deck when she hit the shore. My
head had struck against the inboard end of the bowsprit and
I was only semi-conscious, enveloped by the jib which had
broken its tyers with the force of water and had covered me
completely so that I could neither see nor move, even if I had
the will. But now the hope had been knocked out of me and
I was aware of defeat. Julie crawled up the steeply sloping
deck, pulled the jib away and bent over me.

'Sam, are you all right? Are you hurt? Come and get dry
and warm.'

She helped me to extricate myself and together we made our
way aft along the lee side of the deck. We were out of the wind

but the spray was still flying overhead and the *Rustler* was still jerking and quivering as the waves hit her. The cabin was at an impossible angle and in an impossible mess. Every piece of loose gear had been thrown over on to the lee side—the whole contents of the shelf on the port side were strewn over the floor and over the starboard bunk, Julie's sewing basket had exploded, throwing pins and needles and wool and thimbles over everything. A broken bottle of coffee had formed itself into a sticky brown emulsion on the wet floor, the ship's wheel ashtray had spilled its foul contents on to the starboard bunk. I sat among the chaos while Julie squared up as best she could. Then she bathed a cut on my temple and we struggled into dry clothes. As soon as the tide turned, the wind began to ease, the seas went down and a watery sun came out. At last the *Rustler* lay still and quiet. Some of the watchers from the Promenade came down to the beach again and stood round the boat. We could hear the hum of their conversation, the crunch as they moved on the gravel and the noise of the music from the pier.

It was not nice in the cabin with the boat lying over on her side but Julie managed to make a cup of tea and we sat for an hour in silence, side by side on the starboard settee. Our lives had suddenly come to pieces, our plans were in ruins, even our boat, our home, our only asset, was in jeopardy.

'What are we going to do, Sam?'

'I don't know, I just don't know.'

I felt deflated, tired, dispirited. I knew the next tide would not come near to floating her—would hardly even reach her—I knew that even the next springs in two weeks' time would not provide enough water to get her off. The problem of moving the *Rustler*'s bulk back down the beach towards the water was one which my exhausted intelligence was unable to grapple with. I sat beside Julie in a sort of trance, aware only that a change had come into my life, that the drift of my ambitions and my efforts had been arrested—that in some way I would have to start all over again. A shout from the beach brought me back to the present.

'Julie, are you there?' John came through the companionway, bracing himself against the slope.

'What happened, Julie? How did you get in this mess?'

His eyes darted between us, backwards and forward from Julie's face to mine.

'I thought you were away. Then I came along the front and saw you.'

Julie and I looked at him for a few moments. He seemed nervous, more nervous than usual.

'She was quite all right when I left her,' he said. 'I had to go—I told you I was working at the holiday camp—I was on duty at seven and I had to go—otherwise I'd have got the sack. Sam said he'd be back at four. I waited as long as I could and then at half past six I went ashore. I left the dinghy for you so you could get aboard—left the riding light up. It was quite calm. She was quite all right....'

'If you left the dinghy for me,' I said, 'why wasn't it there when Julie and I came down to the beach just after seven?'

'Not there? Good heavens, of course it was there. It's there still, in the same place.'

'All right, John,' I said. 'Maybe I missed the dinghy in the dark, but how was it that there was five fathoms more chain out and how was it that the anchor was fouled with a half hitch?'

'Anchor fouled? What on earth are you talking about, Sam? How should I know how the anchor got foul? You dropped it, not me. As for the chain—I let it out before I went ashore—standard precaution, old chap. I'm not surprised she dragged in that wind. You ought not to have left her like that, Sam.'

Before I could answer there was a sharp knock against the cabin top. I dragged myself up from the settee, squeezed past John and put my head up through the companion. A man in a blue jacket with brass buttons and a peaked cap had pushed through the crowd. He was a short, round, red-faced man—clean shaven with wisps of fair hair curling out from under his hat like a silvery halo. He looked as if he had just been scrubbed all over with carbolic soap.

'Are you the owner of this vessel, sir?'

'Yes, that's right.'

'Ah,' he said, 'well, sir, I'm the beachmaster. The beach here, all the beach within the confines of the borough that is, sir, is all under my jurisdiction. I'm responsible for it you see, sir—responsible under the bye-laws of the corporation, sir. That is to say, sir, I have to see the beach is properly looked after, that the bye-laws are obeyed, sir, and that there is nothing untoward,' and then he repeated himself, 'nothing untoward, sir.'

He drew himself up and paused in his discourse, looked round the *Rustler*, looked at the people who had clustered round, straining to keep themselves within earshot, and then he pointed up the beach to the red marker buoy.

'The first thing untoward, sir,' he said, 'is that marker buoy. Now that marker buoy is laid for the benefit of vessels plying to and from the piers. From information I have received, I have reason to believe that your yacht was in collision with that buoy and dragged it off its moorings. Is that correct, sir?'

'Yes, that's quite correct,' I said. 'I ran foul of it in the night and that's how I came to be aground on the beach.'

'Ah yes, sir, well that's another matter, sir. I'll come to that next, sir. But first of all the marker buoy. The marker buoy, being the property of the corporation, sir, is also my responsibility and therefore, sir, in the first instance, sir, it will be necessary for you to sign this paper.'

He produced an envelope from his pocket with a flourish, opened it and gave me two closely typewritten sheets of paper. The document started with 'Whereas the Corporation of the City of Brighton ...' and went on to describe the penalties that could be inflicted on anyone who, for any reason, tampered with or otherwise misused the property of the corporation. It said that I would be held responsible for re-laying the buoy, paying for any new equipment that might be necessary, including sinkers, chain, anchors, etc., and paying for the employment of a buoy-laying vessel and possibly the services of a diver. I signed the document and gave it back to him.

'How much will it cost?'

'That, sir,' he said, 'is not my department, sir. But in due course, you will be hearing from the Treasurer's department.'

The beachmaster inspected my signature carefully, folded the two sheets of paper, put them back in the envelope and secreted it in an inside pocket of his jacket.

'The next thing untoward, sir, is this. I have no wish to add to your troubles, sir, but I must point out to you,' he said slowly as if choosing his words carefully, 'that it is not allowed under the bye-laws for vessels to moor on this beach. It is quite untoward. Under the bye-laws,' he said, 'any vessel left on the beach becomes the property of the Corporation. If the owner of the said vessel does not remove it within a stated period of time, the corporation will remove it themselves by whatever means is available to them, and all charges and expenses connected with such removal must be borne by the owner of the vessel.'

'What is the period of time?' I asked him.

'That,' he said, 'is a matter for the Surveyor's department, sir. You will no doubt be hearing from him in due course.'

The beachmaster went off through the crowd with the air of a man who had fired the first shots in what was to be a long battle.

When I went back into the cabin, John said, 'That was old Untoward—a very officious man he is. He used to try and clear us off the beach at night, but we found out that there's nothing in his precious bye-laws to stop us sleeping on the beach. They'll make you shift the boat though, Julie, and if you don't they'll shift her for you.'

'How?' Julie asked.

John glanced quickly from one of us to the other. 'They'll burn her.'

Julie said, 'They won't John—they couldn't.'

95

She turned her big eyes on me. 'There must be a way of getting her off, Sam. Surely we aren't going to sit here and let them burn the *Rustler*? It's unthinkable.'

I climbed out into the cockpit and looked round. It was going to be a beautiful evening. The sun was low and already the sky was preparing itself for a show of splendour. In the west, shafts of pink light were feeling their way round the edges of the stacked clouds transforming them into gigantic grey castles, fringed with red. Overhead the sky was already a clear translucent blue and a few pale stars were coming to life. The wind had dropped to a gentle breeze. The sea had left the *Rustler* and was already halfway down the beach, a few lazy swells tumbling mildly against the shore. There were no more than half a dozen watchers now, standing in a group round the bows.

A man nodded to me. 'Lovely evening now,' he said. 'I suppose you'll have to do a bit of digging to get off here.'

He was right. The *Rustler* would have to be dug out. The bank of shingle on the landward side would have to be shifted back so that the water could get behind her and under her and a deep channel would have to be dug down the beach to allow the tide to flow up to her. It was possible. I had spent enough years of my life shifting earth and gravel to know that it could be done, but I knew that I could never do it by myself unless I could get a bulldozer or a digger down on the beach. I went back to the cabin.

'Nobody's going to burn the *Rustler*,' I said to Julie. 'We're going to get her off at the next spring tides in a fortnight.'

John was sitting beside Julie on the sloping settee. 'I wish you luck,' he said, 'but it looks a pretty impossible task to me.'

I said, 'It's nice of you to wish me luck, John, but all the same I think it would be better if you went ashore now, and quite honestly I'd prefer it if you didn't come back.'

Julie looked at me in astonishment.

John got up and said, 'If that's the way you want it, Sam ...

it's your business, your boat, your problem. All right, I'll go.'
Then, turning to Julie, he said, 'I won't be far off. You know
where to get hold of me if you want me.'

When it got dark I took Julie ashore to have a meal at a
café near the Promenade. The watchers had all gone and
there was no one to be seen on the beach, just a few people
walking along the top of the Promenade, casting curious
glances at the *Rustler*. We went to a pub and had two or
three beers. Julie was upset, more upset than I had ever seen
her and I knew why.

'How can you be certain, Sam? It's a dreadful thing to accuse
him of. I just can't believe that he did it. You're strung up
and you've had no proper sleep for days. You can't really believe
that John fouled the *Rustler*'s anchor deliberately. It's not a
thing anyone would do, least of all John. With all his faults he
does love boats, and anyway ... I don't see how he could have
done it.'

'I'm sorry but I just don't trust him any more. You know
he hates me. You know he hates the idea of our trip. You know
he doesn't want you to go because he needs you here to give
him money. I'm sorry but I just put two and two together.
He was alone on the boat for hours, he could have fouled the
anchor easily—I know it was clear when I dropped it. I just
had a hunch. He's not above stealing to get drugs and I doubt
whether he's above wrecking the *Rustler* to stop his supply of
cash from slipping away from him. These people will do anything—you must know that.'

She wasn't convinced. She couldn't believe it of John. Her
own character was so straight that she hadn't the capacity to
understand deceit in anyone she loved. We sat in the café
until it closed and then we went back to the pub and sat in a
corner talking round and round it, until closing time. In the
end I began to doubt myself. It all fitted in, but there was
nothing to prove it.

'I'm sure you've made a mistake, Sam,' Julie said as we walked
slowly back to the *Rustler* in the moonlight. 'I'm just certain

97

that John wouldn't do that and I think it was wrong of you to accuse him of something you can't prove.'

It all seemed unreal in the moonlight. The nightmare was beginning to deepen and become more horrible. For the first time I felt that the bond of understanding between me and Julie had split apart, allowing an alien discord to creep into the vacuum between us. For the first time we were at odds. We had never had a quarrel since we had been together—hardly a disagreement—and this one went deep. I had hurt her and she was finding it difficult to accommodate the pain. The love we had for each other was wounded and we would be apart from each other until it was mended. We paused in silence for a few minutes on the Promenade, gazing down at the sad, dim outline of the *Rustler* lying on her side on the beach, the brightly lit city behind us and the music from the pier mocked us with a false and hollow gaiety. It was an unreal world which we thought we had shaken off. Instead it held us and was using its perfidious and subtle power to drive us apart. Our escape from it lay stranded and broken on the beach below.

'It's going to be uncomfortable living on board,' I said. 'Maybe you ought to stay in that hotel you were in before, the one near the theatre, until we get her upright.'

'If you're going to stay on board,' she said, 'I'll stay with you. I don't want to leave her.'

We walked down the ramp to the beach and crunched across the gravel. As soon as we got to the boat I saw that something was wrong. The mainsheet was missing. The double block on the boom was hanging empty, the rope had been un-rove and taken away and the boom was resting on the gallows, held only by its own weight. I looked along the deck. The jib sheet and the stays'l sheet were both gone. Julie went straight into the cabin.

'Oh, Sam,' she said when I came in, 'the radio's gone.'

The direction finder was missing from its bracket on the cabin bulkhead, the echo-sounder had been taken from inside the companionway, the binoculars had gone from their stowage, the clock and the barometer had been unscrewed from over the chart table, leaving two round discs of faded paint.

'I didn't lock her up,' I said. 'It never occurred to me.'

I left Julie on board and walked up the beach, looking helplessly in each direction. Then I made my way along towards the West Pier, not knowing why or where I was going, but wanting to be alone. Soon I came to the structure of the pier, looming up in the darkness above me, a tracery of crisscrossed ironwork, damp and festooned with seaweed. There was a hurricane lamp burning against the wall of the promenade under the pier and I could make out the dim shapes of a dozen people huddled in a stone alcove, set into the brickwork. I walked up to them until I stood over the lamp. Some were asleep with old army great-coats drawn over their bodies. Some were smoking pot, others sat with their backs to the brickwork, gazing out at the light with bright, unseeing eyes. A couple had a bottle between them which they passed from one to the other.

'Anyone seen John?' I said.

A young girl sitting between two sleeping forms said, 'He was here earlier on. What do you want?'

She was not old, but her face was lined and ingrained with dirt, her eyes were sunk in her head and her hair hung over her face in matted thongs.

'I've lost some gear and I think he might know something about it.'

There was silence for a moment and then one of the men with a bottle said, 'Fuck off.'

The other one dragged himself to his feet and grasping the bottle, advanced towards me unsteadily. 'Now fuck off,' he said. 'You heard what I said—fuck off out of it.'

I shrugged, walked on out from under the pier and into the clear light of the night, and climbed up a flight of steps on to the Promenade. The music was blaring from the pier, the big dipper roared as the cars came thundering down, amplified voices droned a monologue connected with bingo. For some reason the music put me in mind of Dad sitting in the little room at home, listening to Bach and Mozart—it produced in me a sensation of infinite sadness and nostalgia. There had been security and comfort in those days, now all was brutal and harsh. To lose the *Rustler* would indeed be a harsh and brutal blow. She was everything to me. Without her I was nothing, no more than a labourer on a building site. The *Rustler* contained within her my claim to be a person in my own right. It was the *Rustler* that set me above the ruck. She was the measure of my confidence, the gauge by which I assessed my own worth, the expression of all my endeavours. I could have no quiet, no rest as long as she lay as a hulk on Brighton beach.

I walked across the Promenade, across the road and up into the town. It was late now and few people were about. I found two policemen standing on a corner.

'Report a theft, sir? The police station's just up the road, second on the right.'

While the duty constable was writing the details down in a book an inspector came out of an inner office, glanced at me and then read the report over the constable's shoulder.

'You're the owner of that yacht are you? Bad luck you've had. I saw you trying to get her off. Rotten luck. Now you've had a theft, eh? I'm afraid Brighton's a pretty unruly place at night. Out of our jurisdiction down on the beach, you understand. A matter for the corporation. They have a beachmaster in charge there. But you oughtn't to leave the boat alone for a minute, sir. Lot of bad lots about down there. We'll do what we can of course, but I don't offer much hope of getting the stuff back. You may be in trouble from the corporation before you're much older. I don't think they'll take kindly to the yacht being there for long. They're a pretty unreasonable lot in my opinion, but of course the beach isn't really any concern of mine. We don't go down there unless we're called in by that beachmaster chap.'

'I'll get her off at the next spring tides, Inspector,' I said. 'They must give me as long as that to shift her.'

'I hope so,' he said, and went back into the inner office while the rest of the details were written down. Then the constable slammed the book shut.

'Inspector Parks does a bit of sailing himself,' he said. 'I was with him in the squad car this morning. We were watching you from the Promenade. He reckoned you and the young lady handled the boat pretty well—just bad luck was what he said.'

By the time I got back to the beach the music on the pier had stopped and the lights had gone out. It was high tide now and every vestige of wind had gone. The sea had not even come to the *Rustler*'s keel. It was lapping the shore on the other side of the shingle bank. It was as if she had been picked up by an enormous hand and placed out of her element. I reckoned she would have to be dug down at least four feet before the next spring tide would lift her. Julie had fallen asleep where I had left her, sitting on the lee bunk, her head sunk over her chest, her brown hair hanging down over her face. I got her a pillow from the double cabin, laid her out full length on the settee and put a blanket over her. She still had the pained, hurt expression on her face. She woke as I tucked the blanket round her.

'Where have you been, Sam? Why were you so long?'

'Along the beach to try to find our gear. No luck of course. I went under the pier—where the druggies hang out—but they said they knew nothing about it. Then I asked them if they'd seen John. A pathetic girl told me he'd been around earlier on but had gone off. A couple of drunks started to get aggressive so I went. Then I went up to the police station and reported it.'

'Where are you going to sleep?'

'In the fo'castle on the bench. It's the only place. No one could sleep in our bunk, she's heeled over too much.'

'Put a blanket under you, Sam, and keep warm.'

I kissed her, groped my way into the dark fo'castle and lay down. The *Rustler* was still, like a dead ship. No lapping of water, no gentle swinging on the tide, none of the restless movement which is the life of a ship.

NINE

I was up at dawn and on the first bus to Newhaven, leaving
Julie to keep an eye on the boat and square up as best she
could. As soon as the bus arrived in Newhaven I went to a
small builder's yard at the end of Jubilee Street, next door to
the supermarket. It was a small business, owned by a man who
had known Dad and had known me all my life. I had worked
for him a couple of spells at odd times when he was shorthanded.

'I want to borrow your pick-up truck, Mr Davis. I'll bring it
back this evening.'

He thought for a moment, 'That's all right, Sam. We can
manage without it today.'

Then I went to the yard. Mr Pell was in the office, the room
I knew so well—faded photographs, drawing-pinned to the walls,
the old ship's clock which had never ticked in my lifetime, a
huge bronze bell with s.s. *Minerva* engraved on it, and Mr
Pell's desk made from a lump of mahogany which had come
out of a steamer wrecked on Beachy Head at the turn of the
century. Mr Pell was sitting in his chair, rolling a cigarette,
surrounded by a litter of papers and samples and catalogues,
the Monday morning post, as yet unopened, under his paper-
weight, an enormous lignum vitae sheave.

'Hello, Sam. Didn't expect to see you. Something wrong or
something?'

'Yes, Mr Pell, I'm afraid there is. I've wrecked the *Rustler*.
She drove up on Brighton beach in the gale.'

'Damn it, Sam, you don't say so,' he said. 'I wondered about you in the gale, Sam. I know you left for Shoreham on Wednesday, but I thought you would surely be safely tucked in harbour by Thursday.'

I told him what had happened and he listened without saying a word.

When I had finished he asked, 'Is Missie all right, Sam. Is the boat holed?'

'Julie and I are all right, Mr Pell, and as far as I can see the boat's undamaged except for the bulwarks and stanchions for'ard. She hasn't made any water and I can't see any damage to the hull except a bit of paint rubbed off. We've lost a bit of gear, stolen off her while we were ashore, but I've got to get her off on the next springs and I shall need some help. I wonder if you can lend me some gear and lend me one of the men for a fortnight—Tom or Sid, perhaps? Of course I'll pay for everything.'

'No need to worry about that, Sam. We've known each other a few years. I can lend you anything you need from the yard, but Tom's off sick—in hospital with a hernia, or something. I can't let Sid go. He's working overtime on a job that must be finished in a fortnight.'

We walked round the yard together. I selected a dozen heavy baulks of timber and we loaded them into Mr Davis's truck. I took a big iron block and a coil of two-inch wire, a tin of heavy grease, a short ladder, a hydraulic jack, half a coil of fibre rope, a selection of heavy shackles and a rusty old barge's anchor with the top fluke cut off.

'There used to be an old winch lying up by the gate, didn't there?' I asked him.

'It's still there, Sam. It may be seized up, but it's still there if it's any use to you.'

We had a look at it. It was a heavy affair, which had once been used for hauling out small boats before electricity came to the yard. There was nothing wrong with it. We found the handles for it and hoisted in up into the truck.

'Thanks for everything. I'll let you know how we get on and

I'll return all this stuff as soon as I get her off. I'll have to bring the *Rustler* back to the yard. I'm afraid our trip's off until we get her fixed up again.'

'I'll try and come over and see how you're getting on, or something, in a day or so,' he said.

I set off in the truck, stopping on the way to buy a couple of big shovels and a dozen lengths of softwood in various sizes. Then I went to the bank, changed the travellers' cheques I had bought for the trip back into pound notes and asked the manager to transfer my deposit account money into a current account and make an arrangement to cash cheques at the branch in Brighton. The voyage fund was going to take a knocking but that's what it was for. I could get more money easily enough, but the *Rustler* was irreplaceable.

When I got back to the front at Brighton, there was a throng of people on the beach round the *Rustler*, more than the usual handful of watchers. Julie was standing on the shingle by the cockpit talking to a man in a green pork-pie hat and raincoat. I parked the truck at the bottom of the slope that leads down from the Promenade to the beach and walked across the shingle. The man was writing things down in a notebook in shorthand. There was another man with him, dressed identically, with an expensive-looking camera round his neck.

'Hello, Sam,' Julie said when she saw me. 'This is John Wainwright of *The Brighton Record*. I know him from when I was in the theatre. He wants a story about the *Rustler*.'

'Ah, you'll be Mr Pickson. Now I wonder if you'd tell me exactly what happened in your own words. The whole story of the shipwreck. Of course, we all know Julie Cranbrook. There's bound to be a tremendous lot of interest ... she's pretty well known in Brighton you know ... I've known her for quite a time myself ... used to cover the theatre you know.'

I think he saw my expression because his words tailed off and stopped as if they were operated by a spring which was running out of wind.

'I'm sorry, Mr Wainwright, but I'd rather not say anything.

In fact I'd rather you didn't put anything in the *Record* at all. I just don't want publicity. It was nice of you to come, but, quite honestly, we've got a lot to do and we haven't time to stand around.'

I took Julie's hand and we went inside the cabin.

Julie said, 'Sam, you must be crazy. Why be rude to John Wainwright? He's quite a nice little man. He's certain to put something in the paper anyway. He'll only get the story all wrong if you won't tell him anything. Besides, a bit of publicity might help us. It would certainly help me. You never know, I might want to get another job in Brighton. Why be so unpleasant? The *Record* might even pay you for a story.'

I said, 'Listen, Julie, I hate the idea of being splashed over the *Record* because I've made a bloody fool of myself. I just don't want to know about anything except getting the *Rustler* off this bloody beach and away from this bloody town and away from thieves and drug addicts and theatres and newspapers and the lot.'

Then I calmed down a bit. 'I got a lot of gear from Mr Pell and I borrowed a truck from someone I know in Newhaven. I'm going to start carrying the stuff on board—before someone swipes it out of the truck.'

When I went on the beach, John Wainwright was still there and the photographer was taking pictures of the *Rustler*.

'Do give me a story, Mr Pickson,' he said. 'I shall have to put a story in the paper. Better to get the facts right ... get a full picture of what happened.'

'I'm sorry,' I said, 'no story from me.'

I started carrying to the boat the things I had brought from Newhaven—the wood, the wire, shackles, all the small gear. I stowed it as best I could along the side decks on the port side. I stuck the two shovels side by side in the gravel alongside the boat.

John Wainwright was still hanging about and I heard Julie say to him, 'Sorry, John. If Sam says no story, that's the way it'll have to be. He's the skipper you know.'

When it came to the baulks of timber and the winch I was stumped. I couldn't carry them by myself. I went up to the watchers—there was a lad of about eighteen, a nice-looking boy with curly, fair hair.

'Like to give me a hand?' I said. 'I could do with some help for half an hour.'

Between us, we carried the timber and stacked it on the beach near the *Rustler*'s stern, carried the winch across the shingle and put it on top of the stack of timber.

'Like a job for a few days?' I asked him. 'I'll pay you a pound an hour, but you'll have to work like hell.'

'A quid an hour ... I'll say I would.'

'All right, we'll see how we get on, but I warn you it'll be hard work, bloody hard work.'

We took a shovel each and started clearing the gravel along the *Rustler*'s starboard side, throwing it as far back as we could, making a trench about two feet wide in way of the chain plates. The boy worked well and he knew how to use a shovel.

Julie stopped us at lunchtime and gave us coffee and sandwiches which we ate sitting on the side decks. The boy's name was Jake and he lived just outside Brighton. He was waiting to start a course in engineering at the technical college in Southampton. He'd heard about the *Rustler* being on the beach from his old grandfather who had watched our struggles the previous day and he had come along to have a look.

'Grandad's an old fisherman,' he said. 'He can't keep away from the Prom when it's blowing hard.'

Jake had done a bit of labouring to make money while he was studying. He seemed to know how to work. We started again after half an hour. It was hard. The gravel seemed to run back as fast as you shovelled it out—it was like trying to shovel a hole in the sea. After we had been at it for an hour the beachmaster came along, his peaked cap pulled down over his eyes, the halo of hair, contained at the front, bushed out at the back like a cock's tail feathers. He looked round, embracing at a glance a stack of untoward happenings.

'Ah, Mr Pickson, sir,' he said. 'These timbers here and this winch, sir. Under the bye-laws of the corporation it is not permitted to store gear on the beach. I must ask you to move these articles—forthwith, or sooner, sir.' He paused. 'I understand that truck over there belongs to you, sir. It is not permitted to park vehicles on the approaches to the beach. I will be obliged if you would move it at once.'

'I'm sorry about the truck, beachmaster,' I said. 'If you'll give me half an hour I'll be taking it back to Newhaven. The timber will be put under the boat as soon as we get the digging done. We're doing our best to get her off the beach as soon as possible, you know. The timbers are to help us refloat her. They won't be there long.'

He seemed to be mollified, but he came back with a new and more serious attack.

'I understand,' he said, 'that you and a young lady are living on board the boat. Now this is quite untoward, sir. It is not permitted under the bye-laws to live on board craft moored on the beach and I have been instructed by the Town Clerk to require you to cease doing this at once.'

'But there are dozens of people sleeping on the beach,' I said, 'up there under the West Pier—and as far as I understand it there's nothing in the bye-laws to stop them.'

He was slightly taken aback at this, but he rallied at once.

'That may be so, sir,' he said, 'but sleeping on the beach is not the same as living on board a boat on the beach and it is that, sir, that the bye-laws prohibit.'

Julie had come out into the cockpit and was listening.

'Suppose I went and stayed ashore, beachmaster?' she said. 'Then there would just be Mr Pickson. He'd be acting as a night watchman, wouldn't he?'

The beachmaster glanced up at Julie with what appeared to be a look of relief and gratitude on his pink face.

'That's very reasonable,' he said. 'I think the Town Clerk's department would accept that if I can tell them that's what you intend to do.'

'All right, beachmaster,' I said, 'I give you my word that's what we'll do. I'll stay on board as watchman and Miss Cranbrook will go ashore and live in an hotel.'

I went off to take the truck back, leaving Jake to work on until he got too tired and leaving Julie money to pay him for his labour. Just by the truck there was a large notice which I hadn't seen when I brought it. It said, 'Corporation of Brighton. It is strictly prohibited to bring any vehicle beyond this point in any circumstances.' On the way to Newhaven I called in at the hotel which Julie had been staying in when I first met her in Brighton and booked her a room. I found Mr Davis in his yard. He wouldn't accept any money for the truck.

'We'll say it's for old time's sake, Sam.'

I saw Mr Pell before he went home and told him we had made a start.

'I've managed to get some help,' I said. 'I may need some more before we finish.'

I hitched a lift from Newhaven back to Brighton, but it was dark by the time I got to the *Rustler*. Jake had gone, promising to be back first thing in the morning and the watchers, as usual, had melted away with the coming of darkness. Julie had managed to get some stew going on the sloping galley stove and we had a scratch meal.

She said, 'I'm worried about John, do you think he's sleeping on the beach, Sam? I'm going along to see if I can find him on the way back to the hotel.'

'I shouldn't worry about John,' I said. 'I reckon he's all right. After all he's got plenty of money since you gave him all yours and I suppose after last night he's got a few more pounds tucked away.'

I wished I hadn't said it the second the words were out of my mouth. Julie turned on me, shaking with rage, her eyes shining, her mouth trembling round the corners.

'How dare you accuse John of stealing our things,' she barked at me. 'I thought that was in your mind last night. You haven't a shred of proof. How do you know John did it? You're trying to blame John for everything that's happened. It's rotten of you, Sam—mean and horrible. Even if he did do it, you've got no right to accuse him of it until you've got some proof. Do you think John's a common thief?'

Anger is catching—it feeds on argument, jumps from person to person like a spark, drives out reason, generates bitterness and, when it dies away, it leaves behind resentment, like hot coals in a grate.

'I know he's a common thief. He's told us as much. If he can steal cars he can wreck *Rustler* and if he can wreck the *Rustler*, he can bring up a few of his drugged or drunken cronies and strip her.'

Julie was standing up now, leaning back against the slope, flushed and agitated.

'I'm going,' she said. 'I'm going along to find John, and if I can't find him I'm going back to the hotel.'

She grabbed her bag and her coat, climbed out into the cockpit and jumped on to the shingle.

I rushed out after her, 'Julie, wait a minute. You can't go along there by yourself. Wait a minute and I'll come with you.'

She turned a few paces away from the boat, 'I don't want you to come with me, thank you. I'm perfectly capable of looking after myself,' and she disappeared into the darkness.

I sat alone and lonely in the *Rustler*'s sloping cabin. Before I took up with Julie I had been used to being alone but now it was different. I had got used to her, I had come to rely on her, I needed her, I wanted her. I doubted whether she would come back. Perhaps I was wrong about John. Perhaps Julie's simple faith in him was justified. It was true, I had no proof—a suspicion had taken root in my mind which fed greedily on every chance circumstance, reinforced itself with every flimsy piece of evidence that came its way. John was a pathetic creature in the grip of a weakness that would, in the end, destroy him. Perhaps it was I who had added the malice to his affliction and directed it towards myself. Perhaps I was trying to shift the responsibility for my own misfortunes. The mind slips easily from one evil to another, transporting fact into fantasy, to suit a preconceived notion. If anyone was to blame for what had happened to the *Rustler* it was Julie, but because I loved her I was frightened to associate her with misfortune. It was a deep-rooted fear, born of a guilty awareness somewhere inside myself that she and I should never have come together. After all, I was basically an uneducated labourer. I should never have taken up with her. John was probably right about Mr Cranbrook—he would be horrified that Julie had joined herself with a waif he had picked up in a boatyard all those years ago. He was a liberal man, I knew that, but class goes deeper than opinions—attitudes are dictated by fundamental forces inside people rather than by conscious doctrines. But it was too late. I was in love with her now and love is stronger than reason.

TEN

Jake arrived at eight o'clock in the morning and we set to work at once. By ten we had finished the first part of the digging, a trench two feet wide and long enough to accept the shortest of our timbers, a piece of oak about four feet long. We laid the timber in the trench and placed the hydraulic jack on it, securing it in place with four-inch nails. Then we balanced a timber on the jack, lashed the top of it to the shrouds to keep it steady and secured it to all three chain plates. Jake pumped the jack very gently until we could see that all the lashings were bearing an even strain. Next, we carried our shovels along the beach and down towards the sea to a point immediately abreast of *Rustler*'s mainmast and some twenty yards from it. We just had time to dig a deep hole, sink a timber in it and make a rope fast to it before the tide came up. We led the rope up the beach and made it fast to the *Rustler*'s throat halyard block. We did the same the other side, using the jib halyard and fastening it to a convenient ring bolt in the wall of the Promenade. Now we were ready to hoist her on to an even keel. For once there were no watchers about, but Julie came down the beach just as we were looking for someone to help us. My heart jumped when I saw her—I had convinced myself in my depression that she wasn't going to come back.

'Take this line, darling,' I said to her, giving her the hauling part of the jib halyard, 'and slack it off as she comes up.'

Jake took the hydraulic jack, I took the hauling part of the throat halyard and we started. Jake pumped the jack, I hauled on the halyard with all my strength, while Julie slacked off on hers. *Rustler* began to lift. Everything creaked—the starboard shrouds which were taking the weight of the halyard, the lashings to the chain plates, the gravel under her keel crunched as the weight shifted, but she came up. Soon the jack was at the limit of its upward thrust and Jake let go the lashings. Now she could be lifted without it. The more upright she came the lighter she was, until we had her straight, Julie and I holding her in position with the halyards.

'Sam, that's wonderful,' Julie said.

She was excited, jumping up and down on the beach.

We made the halyards fast to hold her straight. Jake and I took the jack away, moved the horizontal timber to the inside of the trench, so that it was immediately under the chain plates, and lashed another baulk of timber in position as a sheerleg. Then we cleared the ground on the port side, laid another timber in a similar position and lashed the second sheerleg in place. We cut four pieces of the softwood I had brought and nailed them between the tops of the legs and the ends of the timbers on the ground to stop them from shifting. She was safe. We let go the halyards and secured them back in place by the mast. I climbed aboard up the bobstay and lowered down Mr Pell's ladder. Julie and Jake came up.

'This is wonderful,' Julie said. 'Now we're getting somewhere, Sam. I believe we're going to get her off.'

We were all smiling again. Julie made coffee in an upright galley. It was fine to be able to walk about the boat, fine to be able to put things down without them slithering on to the lee side. We put the ship's wheel ashtray back on the cabin table.

'All we want now is some water,' Julie said.

Jake and I had a good look at the hull on the starboard side which had been buried in the shingle. We could see no serious damage—only paint rubbed away all along the turn of the bilge. We went back to digging, stripped to the waist. We started to dig a narrow pit right round the boat, banking the gravel up on either side. We worked at it for three days, until Friday. We would dig down until the bottom of the trench was a few inches below the keel, then we would begin to take the gravel from under the keel itself, working from aft towards the bows. The *Rustler* would settle an inch at a time, by the stern and then we would ease the lashings on the sheerlegs and clear the gravel away from under the bow. Painfully slowly she began to go down until Jake and I were working at the bottom of a deep hole with great heaps of gravel on either side. The tides were low now—neap tides with a smaller rise and fall—and there was a mound of gravel between the *Rustler* and the sea, some that we had thrown up with our shovels and an extra bank that the sea had made, as if to trap the *Rustler* forever in dry dock. The neap tides never came over the bank but the water seeped through so that on our second morning of digging we found a foot of water in the bottom of our trench, making it impossible to work and eroding the steep gravel walls of the pit. We tried bailing it out with buckets, Julie and I and Jake in a line, but it was hopeless. We would have to buy a pump. There was none to be had in Brighton. Julie spent hours on the telephone before she located one in Shoreham. She went off with some money to get it and came back in a taxi with the pump, a length of hose and two five-gallon cans of petrol. I stowed the cans in the forepart of the cabin, out of the way by the door into the fo'castle. The pump kept the water down so that we could work. I prayed that the weather would stay calm, with the wind off shore. Another southerly gale would flood our excavations before we were ready, bring down the shingle banks we had made and undo our work. On Friday we got down to sand, what had once been Brighton beach in the days before the gravel began to build up. We had dug far enough. We cut two of the big timbers into short lengths and dug them in the sand under the keel, first smothering them with grease and then we laid the remaining timbers between the rudder and the shingle bank behind her. Now all we had to do was to clear away the shingle bank at the last moment before the spring tide, and devise a method of pulling her backwards down the beach. We had a week and a day to do it.

Jake and I were exhausted by the digging—Jake was a tremendous worker. I paid him every night because I didn't want him to feel that he had to work until Friday to get his money. This way he could pack up when he liked. I didn't want him to give up, but I knew he would work better that way, without financial coercion. Nobody could be forced to work the way Jake worked. It had come from the heart. He asked if he might bring his grandad down to look at the *Rustler*.

'Grandad knows a lot about pulling boats up and down this beach,' he said.

'Of course you can, Jake. Any time you like.'

We seemed to be spending money like water. The pump cost ninety pounds, I was always sending Julie off to buy something we needed and we got a bill from the corporation for two hundred pounds for re-laying the buoy. The beachmaster brought it down and I wrote him out a cheque. At the same time he told us that we had until Saturday week, until the next spring tides, to clear the *Rustler* off the beach. After that the corporation would take over.

We had trouble with the watchers. They were all right at first, we got used to them. They would try to stop us working to pass the time of day and they would ask questions and make fatuous suggestions. The girls all wanted to pose for a photograph, sitting on the bowsprit and sometimes small boys would slide down the gravel banks of our pit, bringing a shower of small stones with them which we would have to shovel out again, but they were no more than a marginal nuisance to us and we came to regard them with mild affection. On Friday morning *The Brighton Record* came out with a photograph of Julie and the *Rustler* on the front page. 'Actress in Brighton Beach Disaster.' The story was garbled, as I knew it must be—there wasn't line that hadn't got a mistake in it or a glaring howler. 'Julie Cranbrook, well-known star of Brighton Repertory ... grappled with the tiller in huge seas while her brother fought with the shaking spinnaker ... the tiny yacht broached-to against the foaming surf ...' There was a whole page of it. It would have been a riot of fun if it had been about someone else but it brought hundreds of new watchers to the beach on Friday evening and on Saturday. They crowded round the *Rustler* and they began to destroy the banks of our hole, standing on the edge and causing the gravel to collapse inwards, so that Jake and I had to spend hours shovelling it out again. In the end I erected a fence round the boat, tying a rope between pieces of softwood stuck into the gravel. This brought the beachmaster down at once.

'You'll have to take it down, sir,' he said. 'This is a public beach. No one is allowed to make a private enclosure.'

Julie asked the beachmaster to come on board. He climbed up the ladder, took off his peaked cap and sat down on the settee. I gave him a small glass of whisky. At first he refused it but when Julie pressed him he drained the glass and passed it back for another. He was bald on top and without his cap he looked like an enormous, overgrown baby.

'You see, beachmaster,' I said, 'we must keep the trench free of gravel so that when the spring tide comes we can allow the water in to float the boat out. If we let all those people crowd round the top, they'll fill the trench in and we shall be back where we started.'

'You can't fence off the beach,' he said, 'it's untoward,' but a new and softer note had crept into his voice. Julie gave him another whisky. She asked him about his wife, whether he had any children, how long he had been beachmaster. 'I got the job after the war,' he said, 'when I came out of the Navy,' and then added with a touch of pride, 'I was a leading signalman.' Then he went on, 'I could let you have some notice boards I've got in the store, if you would ask your young men to help me carry them.' He went off with Jake and they came carrying large boards on stands with the words Keep Off printed in red letters. We put them up round the boat in place of the fence and the beachmaster was happy.

'How are you going to clear the shingle behind her?' he asked. 'It's more than you and the young man can shift.'

'Don't worry, beachmaster,' I said, 'we'll do it all right when the time comes.'

He looked puzzled and went off.

'How *are* you going to shift that bank, Sam?' Julie asked me in the evening when Jake had gone. The watchers had thinned out and we were alone in the *Rustler*'s cabin. We hardly had any time to ourselves now. Julie went off to the hotel every night. Jake came at eight in the morning and we worked all day, only stopping for half an hour when Julie made lunch for us.

'I'm going to hire a mechanical digger for a day, bring it down here on Saturday, clear the beach behind her in the afternoon at low tide, haul her off on the high tide on Saturday night, that's the biggest tide. For Christ's sake don't tell the beachmaster. It'll make one hell of a mess of his beach and it must be against every bye-law under the sun.'

Julie and I had stopped quarrelling. I think if we had not, I wouldn't have been able to go on struggling with the *Rustler*. She had gone off to find John on Monday night full of bitterness, had walked along to the West Pier and had found him in an almost insensible state, sitting with the others on the gravel with his back against the wall of the Promenade in a coma. She had bent over him and seen the empty syringe on the ground beside him. The rest of them were asleep or in a similar state.

She had tried to get him to go back to the hotel with her, but he had just looked at her with unseeing eyes and said, 'I'm all right, Julie. Just leave me alone.'

In the end she had left him and walked slowly back to the hotel, having half made up her mind to leave Brighton the next day, go back to London and get a job. She had come down to the beach the next morning still in a state of indecision and then she had got caught up in the excitement of getting the *Rustler* upright. We hadn't had a chance to talk about it until evening.

'I'm sorry, Julie,' I said. 'I've been thinking about it all day on and off. I'm sorry. I was wrong to accuse John. I was wrong and you were right. Maybe it was because of everything else—of all the harassment over the last few days—but everything seemed to fit in and point to John. You're quite right. I've no proof. It was just an idea that seemed to get inside me and grow.'

She said, 'John needs help, Sam. He's ill. He's in trouble. It's no use accusing him of things. In any case, I'm just certain he wouldn't have tried to harm us like that.'

I agreed that we should both go and try to find John the next day. I promised to apologize to him, to tell him he could come on board the *Rustler* whenever he liked. Julie said she would find out whether he still had his job. We would try to help him get straight, get himself some digs and maybe persuade him to go to a clinic. There is nothing so sweet as reconciliation. Julie's big eyes became soft pools of sympathy, the resentments dropped away like a stage set, the recriminations evaporated. We lay together in the *Rustler*'s double cabin, our minds and our bodies merged into one, our small world overtaken by perfection, our concepts of beauty brought together into an immediate understanding of absolute happiness. We stayed together for a long time. In the dim light of the cabin I gazed into Julie's eyes, gazed through them, past the light brown fleck and into the recesses of her mind, finding truth and contentment.

'You must go home,' I said to her, 'or we will have the beachmaster after us.'

The next morning when Julie came back from the hotel we went together to find John, leaving Jake to run the motor pump until the hole round the *Rustler* was dry and then to carry on with the ceaseless digging.

117

'I won't be gone longer than I can help,' I said, 'not more than half an hour.'

There was no sign of John under the pier, only the girl I had seen before and a young man with long hair. They seemed to be gathering up their belongings into bundles and stacking them beside the wall. There were several other bundles of odd clothes and belongings laid out neatly beside the wall as if the owners had claim to a permanent position.

The girl said, 'Who wants to know?' when Julie asked where John was.

'I'm his sister,' she said. 'I wanted to speak to him, that's all.'

She directed us to a café in the town, near the front, 'You may find him there,' she said, 'or there again you may not.'

It was a small place, not very clean, with a row of tables down one side and a long counter with a steaming, hissing coffee machine and cardboard plates with hairy looking buns for sale, on the other. Over the door was a big sign with 'S.P.O. – chips' written in big red letters. John and three others were sitting in the far corner, beyond the counter, drinking cups of turgid-looking tea.

'Hello, Julie,' John said when he saw us. 'I thought I was never going to see you two again. Thought you'd given me the brush-off for good. Have a cup of tea.'

I declined but Julie said she would.

'One cup of tea, Horatio,' John shouted to a crone behind the counter. 'Make it a clean cup. We've got gentry with us,' and then he said to Julie, 'Her husband's called Nelson.'

John was in good form. He shot glances at Julie and I out of black-rimmed, hollow eyes. I felt awkward.

'I'm sorry for what I said the other night, John—or rather for what I implied. I was a bit het-up, anyway. Come back on board whenever you like.'

'Good heavens,' he said, 'I thought I was barred. All right, Sam, no hard feelings,' and he proffered his hand.

I shook it. 'No hard feelings.'

Then I made an excuse and went back to the *Rustler*, while

Julie stayed in the café with her cup of tea. As I walked back across the Promenade I couldn't escape the feeling that I'd made a fool of myself in front of John yet again. I couldn't shake off that first hunch. John could always make me feel an inch high. At least Julie and I were friends again. Nothing was worse than quarrelling with Julie—any price, even weakness, capitulation if you like, was worth paying for her.

Julie came back to make our lunchtime sandwiches and coffee. That evening, when Jake had gone, she told me about John.

'He's got another job—at the Lido—swimming instructor. He'll be there till the end of the month when the season closes. He has got digs and he promised me he'd go back there to-night. He said he was going to pack up drugs—said he'd stick to grass—he says it's harmless and I suppose it is really. He swore to me he'd never take heroin again.'

I didn't say anything. John came on board later and we all had supper together in the *Rustler*'s cabin.

'You've dug a hell of a big hole for her, Sam,' he said. 'How are you going to get the shingle away from her stern?'

'Sam's got it all worked out,' Julie said. 'He's going to get a mechanical digger—one of those great big things with caterpillar tracks and sweep the whole lot away next Saturday morning, when the tide's low. We're going to get her off on the spring tide on Saturday night.'

I could have bitten her head off but instead I bit my lip and said nothing.

'Don't, for God's sake, breath a word about it,' she went on. 'If the beachmaster got to hear of it, he'd come down on us like a ton of bricks.'

'Good heavens,' John said.

ELEVEN

I telephoned Mr Pell on Saturday morning and asked him if he had a new chain roller for the anchor cable. I had forgotten to mention it when I had seen him at the yard. In fact I had forgotten about the anchor altogether.

'I'll bring one over this afternoon, Sam. I wanted to come over and see how you were getting on anyway.'

Jake and I had finished clearing the gravel away from round the hull and the *Rustler* lay in a deep hole, surrounded by steep shingle banks. The problem was to keep the hole from filling in. Shovelling gravel was a job with no end. As fast as you threw it out, it came rattling down the banks from somewhere else. Sometimes the watchers would penetrate the beachmaster's notices and when they came to the edge of the pit, gravel would run down into it like a miniature waterfall. If the hole got filled up again, we wouldn't have a chance. If the tide got into it before we were ready, it would demolish our pit and leave the *Rustler* as hard and fast as she had ever been. Jake used the motor pump for three hours every day. If we could keep the hole dry, when we did demolish the bank behind her and made a channel down the beach, she should move out easily. I reckoned we had dug her down nearly far enough— nearly four feet—but the gale had thrown her up at least three feet above high water and next spring tide fell short of the previous one by nearly a foot. Everything depended on the weather and on having a good tackle to pull her off the shore. Mr Pell arrived in the afternoon, bringing with him a good, strong chain roller, a bag of tools and four galvanized bolts to fasten the roller to the stem. He came on the bus. Mr Pell would never have a car—he hated them.

'Better if everyone went a bit more slowly,' he would say.

He looked at the damage to the bulwarks and stanchions on the foredeck.

'She'll have to come into the yard,' he said. 'Top strake's come away and the covering board's split. I reckon she's a strong old boat, Sam. Most of 'em would have broken up, or something.' He looked at the great mound of shingle behind her. 'You'll need some help to shift that lot, Sam,' he said. 'I can't see you and Missie and this young chap here doing it.'

I told him about the digger.

'Well,' he said, 'it might work ... but how are you going to fix the winch in position? Nothing to bed it down on.'

It was the very thing that I had been worrying about—the one weak point in what seemed a sensible plan. I had thought the job out in my mind. I would put Mr Pell's big barge anchor down as far out as I could get it, attach the iron block to it and lead the wire from the *Rustler*'s stern, out to the anchor and back up the beach to the winch. I thought I would secure the winch in position by digging in upright baulks of timber and marrying them together with a crosspiece to set the front edge of the winch against. I thought I might help hold the winch in position by taking another wire to a ring-bolt in the wall of the Promenade, but at best it was a ramshackle arrangement. That afternoon, after Mr Pell had fixed the chain roller and all of us were sitting in the cabin having a cup of tea, we had a stroke of luck—at least you could call it that if you believed in luck. The play of chance had been against us for so long that it was ready for a swing the other way. Jake's old grandfather came down to see us.

Jake's grandad was eighty-six but he climbed nimbly up the *Rustler*'s ladder. He had a short, grey beard, a shock of silver hair and piercing blue eyes. Mr Pell knew him well—he had known him all his life.

'Well, if it isn't old Harry Seccombe,' Mr Pell said. 'I thought you were dead years ago.'

'Well, that's a nice thing to say to an old fisherman, ain't it? I reckon I'll outlive half of you young buggers.'

We gave him a cup of tea and he started telling us about the old days. I didn't really want to spend time listening to Harry, but he was a charming old boy and I didn't want to offend Jake, who had asked me specially if he might bring his grandad down to see the *Rustler*.

'Time was when there was thirty luggers workin' off this 'ere beach,' he said. 'Boats about the size of this one—only they didn't 'ave keels or nothing—leeboards they had and some of 'em had centreboards. Mind you, there was bigger boats afore the luggers—the old Brighton "hoggies"—but that was before all this shingle came. They built them groynes when the place started to get smart, 'cause they thought the sea was going to take the cliffs away. Of course that was before they built this 'ere Promenade. Then the gravel started acomin' in and laid over the sand—so then we had to heave the old boats up the beach with capstans and heave 'em back in the water with blocks and bloody great anchors off the beach. Why, there was thirty luggers aworkin' off of this 'ere beach when I was a boy—ask Burt Pell if there wasn't. His dad used to repair 'em.'

'That's right,' Mr Pell said. 'In my father's day, before there was much in the way of yachts, we worked on the fishing boats all year round.'

'You'd see 'em come up the beach in a hard blow,' Harry went on. 'The hands would be round 'em, the bow line would be thrown over the capstan and they'd be up above the high-tide mark inside ten minutes. I've had 'em off in a hard blow too,' he said slyly, 'if there was any salvage about—ship ashore off Beachy or Selsey or 'owt like that. Why, there was one of them old capstans not ten yards from this spot, covered up wi' shingle now, of course, but still there right enough.'

I was suddenly interested.

'What sort of capstans were they, Harry?'

'Why, they was big old wooden capstans, set in great stone blocks they were, buried right down deep in the sand. Of course the wood part's all gone now, but the stone bed's still there I'll warrant.'

'Can you point out exactly where the capstan was, Harry?'

'Why, of course I can,' he said. 'I ought to know where the bugger is. This one here was where the *Maid* was hauled up.'

Jake and I went ashore, grabbed our shovels and Harry stood in the *Rustler*'s cockpit and told us where to dig.

'Little bit to the east'ard,' he said. 'Down to the sea a bit.'

He came ashore, took his bearings off a ring bolt in the Promenade and the corner of a flight of stone steps and said, 'There, that'll be about four foot down, I reckon.'

Harry went back on board to his cup of tea and his yarn with Mr Pell while Jake and I got to work. A few of the watchers detached themselves from the main group round the *Rustler*'s bow and came to have a look.

'Looking for gold?'

'No, stone.'

Jake and I worked as hard as we could for an hour and, just as we were giving up, Jake's shovel hit the stone. Julie came out into the cockpit when she heard my shout of triumph. She jumped ashore and peered into the hole we had dug. Right at the bottom, when Jake moved the stones away with his shovel, there was a hard base.

Julie said, 'Sam, this is wonderful. Harry says there's an anchor with a heavy chain on it off shore to take the block. He says he knows where that is too. He's fantastic, Sam.'

Harry and Mr Pell came over and peered into the hole.

Harry said, 'You clear that old stone away with your shovel and I reckon you'll find two big pieces o' timber set in that. Now, you could fasten your winch to them, easy.'

I asked him about the anchor off shore.

'Take a line off that there church spire and the corner of the Promenade. Take another line from the old water tower through that there chimney, and where they meet, you'll find the anchor. Mind you, that may be covered up wi' shingle now, but I'll reckon you'll find it. There ain't so much shingle down below the tide—there's still sand down there. There'll be about four and a half feet of water over it at low tide.'

Julie said, half unbelieving, 'How can you remember so exactly, Harry?'

'Remember?' he said. 'Damn it, Miss, I ought to remember. It ain't mor'n forty years since I laid the bugger.'

Mr Pell and Harry went off, Mr Pell to catch his bus back to Newhaven and Harry to his tea. It was nearly dark, Jake knocked off for the night and the watchers dispersed.

'That was a bit of luck, Julie,' I said. 'As far as I can see the anchor's in exactly the right position. So is the winch come to that. Might've been put there specially for us. Good old Harry.'

We went on board, lit the cabin stove and Julie began to get a meal ready. John came when we were halfway through.

'I see you've dug another hole. What are you going to put in it?'

'The winch,' Julie said, and she told him about Harry and the anchor.

'What are you going to do when you get her off? Where are you going to take her?'

'Back to Newhaven,' Julie said. 'She'll go back to the yard. Mr Pell's going to fix the stanchions and bulwarks and she's got to be hauled out to have a look at the bottom and give her some more paint. Then we'll be off.'

'Where to?'

'Why, the trip, of course. You didn't think we'd change our minds did you?'

'I didn't think you'd go in the middle of winter,' he said. 'That's a bit risky isn't it?'

'We may wait till the early spring,' I said. 'We'll see how the jobs go and see how much money we've got left. But we'll certainly go as soon as we can get away.'

John was silent for a few minutes and then he said, 'I would have thought after this experience you'd give it a miss. I've never thought much of the idea, as you know. But now you've seen how much trouble you can get into, I would have thought it best to change your minds.'

'Never,' Julie said.

John pulled an old tobacco tin out of his pocket and rolled himself a cigarette, mixing the tobacco with some weed out of another tin. You could smell the marijuana as soon as he lit it. I looked at Julie uneasily.

'I don't think you ought to smoke that stuff here,' I said. 'If anyone comes on board we might all get into trouble.'

'Don't be such a bloody puritan,' John said. 'The stuff's quite harmless—better for you than cigarettes any day.'

Julie shrugged and looked concerned, but she didn't say anything. I went into the fo'castle and started sorting out some gear we would need the next day.

It took Jake and I most of Sunday to clear the gravel away from the capstan bed, to clear a space round so we could work the winch handles and to smooth out the gravel in front so that the wire would lead direct out to the anchor. We found two heavy pieces of timber fastened to the stone in some way, which must have been there for generations. It happened that the distance between them allowed Mr Pell's winch to sit neatly in position. We would be able to fix it down with four big coach screws. On Monday morning when the tide was low, we found the chain from Harry's anchor. It wasn't difficult. Jake sculled me out in the dinghy to the point off the shore where old Harry's two leading lines crossed. There was exactly four foot six of water, as Harry had said. I went over the side and stood on the bottom, steadying myself with the dinghy. Exactly where the lines crossed, my feet came into contact with something solid. It was a huge link of chain sticking up out of the sand bottom. It was so heavy and solid that I couldn't shift it but there was enough of the link clear of the bottom to be able to shackle on Mr Pell's big iron block, bending down under the water and holding my breath for as long as I could. Then we uncoiled the length of wire, passed an end through the block, took it to the winch and fastened it to the drum. The other end just reached to the *Rustler*'s stern. It seemed that everything was working in our favour. Jake and I started to make a rope sling to go round the *Rustler*'s hull.

On Tuesday I put on a decent pair of trousers and went in a taxi to arrange for the digger. I went to a firm of plant hire contractors outside Lewes. I had been there dozens of times and knew the manager.

'You mean you want to hire a digger for yourself, Sam? What are you going to do, dig the garden?'

There wasn't a digger to be had, only a bulldozer.

'You'll need a low loader to take it down there and bring it back. Do you know what it's going to cost you, Sam?'

'You tell me.'

He thought for a moment, 'At least a hundred quid.'

'That's about what I thought.'

'Cash in advance, Sam.'

I had a job to persuade him to let me drive the bulldozer and the loader myself.

'I've been doing it for years. You know that as well as I do.'

'It's not that, Sam. Of course I know you can do it. But it's a bit irregular, you know. Normally your firm takes the responsibility, you know, insurance and all that.'

We were standing in the site office, a wooden hut with a high desk covered in papers. I took two ten pound notes from my pocket and slid them across the desk. He looked at them.

'Perhaps we could do it a bit unofficial,' he said as he slid the notes into his pocket. 'You know, a bit of a deal between you and me. There won't be anyone much about on Saturday afternoon. I could have the 'dozer loaded up ready. You come for it at two o'clock. I'll be here. You can bring it back at five.'

I gave him another thirty pounds in notes.

'I'll give you the rest when I see you on Saturday, another fifty.'

'All right, Sam, but I'm taking a hell of a risk, you know. If anything goes wrong with this I'll lose my job.'

'There's nothing to go wrong as far as I can see.'

I told Julie about it when we were alone on board in the evening.

'A hundred pounds, Sam. That's a vast sum of money.'

'It's cheap. If we did it officially, it would be much more. A driver for the 'dozer, a driver for the low loader, all at over-time on Saturday afternoon. It'd cost a bomb. It'd cost as much if we cleared the shingle with labour, even if we could get the people to do it.'

'I hope he sticks to his word,' she said, 'or we're done for.'

'Don't worry, he will. It's the beachmaster I'm worried about.'

The weather gave me a bad scare on Wednesday. It blew a short, sharp gale. It had been perfect ever since we went on the beach, nothing but blue skies, wonderful starlit nights, misty mornings and a gentle but cold easterly breeze. On Wednesday the sun rose in an oily, threatening sky, the wind swung round to the south-west and it was blowing a gale by mid-morning. The waves began to build up on the beach. They almost came over the shingle bank behind the *Rustler* but not quite. Jake and I kept the motor pump going all day and in the evening the gale subsided as quickly as it had come. I was glad we had not spent the last ten days trying to clear a channel between the *Rustler* and the sea. The gale would have undone our work in a couple of hours. As it was, the bank of gravel across the *Rustler*'s stern was made even larger by the gale. She was sitting in a deep hole surrounded by gravel, like a Viking ship excavated from a burial mound. On Thurs-day, Jake and I fixed Mr Pell's winch on its bed with four massive coach screws which bit into the old timber bed and gripped the winch solidly in position. We finished the rope sling round the *Rustler*'s hull, tying her up like a parcel, so that she could be pulled out stern first, with the strain taken evenly by a cat's cradle of ropes. We seized in a big shackle and made the wire fast to it by doubling the end back into an eye which we fastened with bulldog grips. The beachmaster couldn't disguise his curiosity.

'Of course, sir, you'll be moving all this gear off the beach as soon as you've got the boat off, sir.'

'Of course, beachmaster,' I said. 'I'll come in a truck on Monday morning and take it all away. In a couple of days there'll be nothing to show we were ever here.'

As time went on and he saw us make no effort to tackle the small mountain of gravel behind us, he became more and more puzzled.

'You'll need a lot of men to shift all that stuff behind her, sir.'

'Don't worry, beachmaster, we'll clear it.'

He went off, half-convinced that something untoward was afoot, that in some way an attempt was to be made to force a breach in the bye-laws. Inspector Parks came to see us on Friday. We asked him on board.

'I'm afraid there's no sign of your stolen gear,' he said. 'We've made all the routine inquiries, but nothing's come to light.'

He had been watching our work day by day from the Promenade.

'You seem to have made a good job of getting everything ready,' he said. 'The only thing I don't understand is how you're going to shift all that shingle.'

I explained to him why we hadn't made any attempt to clear a channel to the sea.

'That last gale would have wrecked it anyway,' I said. 'The only way to do is to wait till the low water before the spring tide and then to shift the lot.'

'You'll need an army of men,' he said, 'unless you're going to use a bulldozer.'

'That's exactly what I am going to do, Inspector, on Saturday afternoon.'

'I see,' he said. 'That explains it. Has the beachmaster agreed to this?'

I told him I had been scared to mention it, 'I just know he would raise every type of objection. He'd never allow it.'

'Well, if he sees you at it he may try to stop you. Of course, if he calls in the police, we would have to act. He'd be perfectly within his rights to call us in if the law was being broken and I have no doubt that what you propose doing is against the law.'

'If we had a bit of time,' I said, 'no more than a couple of hours, we could get it all done. After that they can summons me if they want to and I'll pay the fine gladly.'

'Well,' he said slowly, 'sometimes the police are pretty quick off the mark and sometimes—well you know—the wheels of the law take a bit of time to start moving.'

Jake and I rove off a new mainsheet from a spare coil of rope I had in the fo'castle and we made new sheets for the jib and stays'l. We recovered our two anchors and stowed the chain back in the locker. We checked over all the sails and cordage and we ran the engine for a few minutes to make sure everything was in order. Jake was worth his weight in gold. He not only knew how to work but he knew his way about a boat. John was often aboard. He seemed to have given up sleeping under the pier. He seemed to have shaken off his shady friends and to have come off heroin, at least for the present. He had always maintained that he was not addicted, that he could take it up and put it down at will. I doubted whether this was possible but Julie believed him. She had more faith than I had, not only about John but about everyone. His job at the Lido would end on Sunday and he said he was going to London to look for work. Julie was delighted.

'He's going to be all right, Sam,' she said. 'All he needs is sympathy and kindness. If only he could meet some nice girl and get himself a real purpose in life he'd be fine.'

It seemed as if, at last, everything was going to work out. If I could get even a couple of hours with the bulldozer, I knew

I could shift enough gravel to allow the water to flow round the *Rustler*. Even if she didn't float on the top of the tide there was enough power in the winch to drag her off and once afloat, we would run for Newhaven as fast as the sails or the engine would take her. We had plenty of petrol in the tanks and if the worst came to the worst and we ran out, the two five-gallon cans for the motor pump were almost full. Julie was bubbling over with good spirits.

'We'll start all over again, Sam. Mr Pell will get the *Rustler* fixed up in no time. We'll both work and we'll save money like mad, and we'll set off again and forget all about this business, just as if it was some horrible dream.'

I loved her for her optimism. I loved her for bouncing back after a knock, I loved her because she was a part of me—the best part—pulsating with hope and courage, throbbing with vitality, doubly blessed with beauty and with a soft heart. All the same, I remember that somewhere inside me was a tiny needle of anxiety, pricking away with painful jabs of doubt.

TWELVE

I didn't sleep well that last night on Brighton beach. I turned in after Julie left to go back to the hotel but things kept going round and round in my head. The music from the pier, the light rain that was falling outside, the noise of cars on the Promenade, the soft surge of the sea on the beach, all combined to produce a feeling of unease, an eerie sensation of disquiet. Once I heard the crunch of someone walking along the shingle. I jumped out of bed and into the cockpit but the footsteps grew fainter in the direction of the pier. Probably one of the druggies going home to his inhospitable bed—what a life that must be. I made myself a cup of tea and sat in the cabin for an hour—the *Rustler*'s happy, familiar cabin, lit by an oil lamp, Julie's picture on the bulkhead, the ship's wheel ashtray on the table, the thumbed and grubby books, the vacant circles on the paintwork where the clock and the barometer had been, the cushion that Julie had covered, the kettle, sitting on the stove and poking its snout in the air like the village idiot. I had a strange feeling of nostalgia. It was as if I was looking at all this for the last time.

I thought about Dad sitting in the old armchair by the fire in Jubilee Street while the music filled his mind with a world of fantasy. I wondered whether Dad had loved Mum as much as I loved Julie. After she died, he had almost ceased to be a person. He had retreated into the music like a small, hurt animal, burrowing into the ground, only emerging when the pain became unbearable and there was nothing for him but to make himself drunk. Poor old Dad. I suppose, if I lost Julie, I might do the same. I went to bed and tried again but the roundabout went on. I twisted myself this way and that. I went through all the uncertainties, grappled with imaginary problems. There was a picture in my mind's eye of the *Rustler* riding securely to her anchor, trim and neat, in all the glory of her natural grace and dignity. At the same time the old feeling of doubt grumbled and complained and worried at the frayed edges of my confidence. At last the dawn brought a release from the prison that was my imagination.

It wasn't much of a day. A thin drizzle fell with consistent ill will from a low, windless sky, making the world into a damp, gloomy place. Even the music from the pier was muted and melancholy. A seagull sat on Mr Pell's winch surveying the *Rustler* with bored disinterest. Jake was the first to arrive, breaking the pall of despondency with his natural cheerfulness.

'Well, this is the day, Sam. I'll be out of a job tomorrow.'

'No harm in that, Jake. You've earned a rest the way you've worked for the last ten days.'

'I've enjoyed it. Somehow I've got fond of the *Rustler*. I think I understand something of what you feel about her. I can't wait to see her afloat.'

We went round in the rain checking everything that was to be done. We took a few turns on the winch, watched the strain come on the wire and checked that the rope sling round the hull was taking an even pull. Then we disconnected the wire from the sling and from the winch, carried the two ends clear of the *Rustler*'s stern and left them loose on the beach so that the bulldozer would be able to work without fear of fouling them. Julie came down early and made us coffee, bringing her suitcase from the hotel.

'I've got to go back there, Sam. I haven't paid the bill. You forgot to give me any money.'

'Plenty of time for that,' I said. 'It's not as if we're going far away.'

She wanted to come with me to fetch the bulldozer.

'Of course you can come, darling. Jake can stay with the boat.'

It was still raining but I didn't mind—it kept the watchers away. The beachmaster came along at eleven, wearing a long oilskin coat over his reefer jacket. It was high tide and the sea was lapping the top of the shingle bank. The motor pump was running hard, keeping the seeping tide away from the *Rustler*'s hole.

'Going off today, sir?' he asked.

'On the tide tonight, beachmaster.'

He looked doubtfully at the shingle bank.

'Got a gang of men coming I suppose, sir,' he said. 'It'll take a bit of shifting that lot.'

'Something like that, beachmaster,' I mumbled.

'You'll be clearing all this stuff off the beach I suppose, sir.'

'On Monday morning, beachmaster, as I promised.'

He produced an ancient duplicate book from the pocket of his oilskin, wrote out a form, tore it out of the book and gave it to me.

'Beach dues, sir,' he said, 'one pound and four pence.'

I gave him the money and he disappeared in the direction of his hut by the Palace Pier, pausing to look at the two bare ends of the wire lying at the edge of the sea with an expression of infinite puzzlement in his baby-blue eyes. John was our next visitor.

'Nothing doing at the Lido because of the rain,' he said. 'I'm off to London tomorrow. I just thought I'd come to see how you were getting on.'

'Sam and I are going off to get the bulldozer in a minute,' Julie said. 'The beachmaster's in a hell of a twitter. He can't make out what we're going to do.'

John went off saying he'd be back later. Julie and Jake and I had a snack lunch in the *Rustler*'s cabin.

We went off to Lewes just after one.

Before going, I said to Jake, 'I'll be back at about quarter past two. You'll see the loader over the top of the Promenade. Don't let anyone on board, Jake—anyone.'

I had a good look at the layout of the pavement at the top of the ramp which leads down to the beach. There was a shallow lay-by in the road. I could fit the loader neatly into it and drive the 'dozer straight on to the pavement and then down the ramp to the beach. Julie and I found a taxi and drove to the plant contractor's yard outside Lewes. I paid the driver and told him to be back at half past five. The loader was drawn up outside the site office with the bulldozer already on it, fastened down to the ring bolts with bottle screws and clamps. The manager was in the office. I counted out fifty pounds in fivers and he rolled it up and put it in his pocket. I checked over the loader and the 'dozer, making sure that there was fuel and that the ramp on the loader was working properly. It was a routine I had been through a hundred times.

'See you at half past five.'

'All right, Sam, watch it boy. If anything goes wrong with this, I'm out.'

Julie climbed into the cab and perched herself high up on an old cushion beside me. I pressed the starter and the engine roared. We swung out on to the road and trundled towards Brighton. It was still raining softly. No harm in that. It might keep the beachmaster at home. Nobody in their senses would wander about a beach on an afternoon like this. Julie was excited, like a kid out in a car for the first time.

'Sam, you're wonderful. What a thing to drive, it's enormous.'

I approached the town from the east, driving slowly along the front. There wasn't much traffic on a wet Saturday afternoon—with any luck the beachmaster wouldn't even see us. The rain suited me well. When we got to the Metropole I stopped the loader, got out and undid the clamps on the 'dozer. I didn't want to waste time when I got to the ramp. I left Julie in the cab and walked along to the lay-by. As I had feared, there was a car right in the middle of it—a man and his wife looking at the rain-swept sea and at the top of the *Rustler's* mast. I knocked on the window.

'Excuse me, sir, there's a loader with a bulldozer coming in here. Would you mind moving along please?'

'Not at all,' he said, and he drove slowly away.

I went to the edge of the Promenade to call Jake and then I saw trouble in front of me—lots of trouble.

The beachmaster was down by the boat having a tremendous argument with Jake. The 'Keep Off' notices had all been carried up the ramp and had been place across the top like a row of soldiers. A chain had been put up across the top of the ramp from the inner wall of the Promenade to one of the iron railings and fastened with a big padlock. I ran back to the loader and climbed into the cab.

'We've been rumbled,' I said to Julie. 'The beachmaster's up in arms.'

'What do you mean?'

'You'll see.'

I let in the clutch and drove along to the lay-by, parking the loader with its back end against the curve of the pavement. I pulled a lever, there was a hiss of compressed air, and the sloping back of the loader dropped smoothly down on to the pavement.

'Go down to the boat, Julie,' I said. 'Keep him talking. Don't leave him for a moment. Try and keep him on the beach. Don't let him get to the police station.'

She ran off. I climbed up into the 'dozer's seat and pressed the starter. I had a bird's eye view of the *Rustler*. I saw the beachmaster turn when he heard the bulldozer's engine roar into life. I saw Julie running down the beach towards him. Then I let in the clutch and manoeuvred the 'dozer down off the loader, across the pavement with its enormous scoop hard up against the chain. I looked round—there wasn't a policeman to be seen—in fact there was no one to be seen on the front. I blessed the rain. As I let in the clutch the beachmaster came running up to the bottom of the ramp, pursued by Julie and Jake. I raised the scoop a foot off the ground and let the huge machine creep slowly forward. The chain came bar-tight as the scoop pressed against it, the iron stanchion began to bend, then there was a crack as the chain broke, the ends flying back as if released by a spring. I lowered the scoop to the ground and as the 'dozer moved down the ramp, the 'Keep Off' notices tumbled in front of it and were swept on their sides towards the beachmaster who was standing shouting in the middle of the ramp.

'Clear off, beachmaster,' I yelled above the noise of the engine. 'Get lost.'

He retreated towards Julie and Jake at the bottom. I turned the machine at the bottom, shook the wooden notices free of the scoop and moved the bulldozer slowly towards the *Rustler*. The noise of the engine was thrown back by the stone walls of the Promenade, the caterpillar tracks dug into the gravel and the machine moved across the beach like a huge mechanical slug. The beachmaster came running beside the cab.

'You can't do this,' he shouted. 'I'll have the law on you. It's against the bye-laws to bring a vehicle on this beach. The corporation won't stand for this. You can't get away with this ... untoward action ... sir.'

'Speak to the young lady,' I shouted back at him. 'She knows all about it.'

I switched my mind off the beachmaster and left him to Julie and Jake. I needed all my concentration and I would have to work fast. The first sweep I took was diagonally across the *Rustler*'s stern, as close to it as I could get. The engine of the bulldozer roared and black smoke spewed from its exhaust as it felt the strain. The gravel built up in a great mound over the scoop as the machine pushed it back like a tidal wave. I pushed the first lot well clear of the *Rustler*'s stern and then I brought the machine backwards and set it at the gravel mountain once more. The tracks were slipping a bit on the loose surface—I had to be careful not to let the machine take too much weight. If it bogged it would be the finish. In four sweeps I had got down to sand, the same level as the *Rustler*'s keel. The beach was beginning to look like a battlefield. I saw out

of the corner of my eye that the beachmaster was halfway up
the ramp, still arguing hotly with Julie while Jake stood to one
side. She was waving her arms about and shouting at the top
of her voice and the beachmaster was trying to push past her.
Julie was putting on a tremendous act—it was her job after
all. I took another great swathe out of the gravel beside the
first one, and then repeated it three times until I had cleared
a hole big enough to take the bulldozer itself. Now I could
turn the machine towards the sea and sweep the gravel down
the beach. When I looked round I saw the beachmaster at the
top of the ramp, still with Julie screaming at him. Jake left them
and came running down the beach.

'He's going to the police,' Jake said, 'but Julie's doing a
terrific act with him—she's throwing hysterics at him.'

'Fine,' I said. 'Get a shovel Jake and clear out the gravel
from round her stern. I can't go too close with the 'dozer and
I've spilled a bit.'

There was still a narrow ridge behind her, where the edge
of the scoop had swept past. Now I had the machine facing
the sea and I was clearing a wide path down to the low water
mark. I didn't dare go too close to the sea—the ground was
soft down there, only a thin layer of gravel, then sand, then
mud probably, and the 'dozer weighed tons. I had gone far
enough. I turned and swept back towards the *Rustler*, pushing
a vast mountain of gravel up on either side of a wide cut. The
engine of the 'dozer was roaring and belching smoke, the great
machine was bucking and swaying and shuddering under the
weight of gravel and the beach was being bisected by a deep
canal from the *Rustler* to the sea. I had always liked working
with a bulldozer—I never got tired of it in all the years I did
it. It was a job where you were left on your own to work it
out as you knew best and a job where you could see the results
of your labour.

I was just about finished when Julie came back.

'He's in the police station. I couldn't stop him going, but I
made it as hard as I could. We had a scene in the middle of

the road, stopping all the traffic. You know the stuff, four starving kids and a drunken husband ... he was so embarrassed, poor man. Inspector Parks is writing all the details down in a book. He's not hurrying but they'll be here inside half an hour.'

It was nearly low tide now and I had made a wide, deep channel from the *Rustler*'s stern, almost down to the sea, four feet below the level of the beach. For the first time you could see the boat from seaward instead of a bank of gravel with a mast sticking up behind it. I manoeuvred the machine up out of the channel I had made and drove it towards the ramp. It had done a magnificent job. A wide slice of beach had been cut away, but I knew that in a short time the sea would level it all out again.

Julie came and helped me guide the 'dozer back up the ramp and on to the loader. We had just got it settled in position when two constables came along the Promenade with the beach-master.

'You, Mr Pickson, sir?'

'Yes, Officer.'

'We've had a complaint from the beachmaster that you've been using some earth-moving equipment on the beach, which is against the bye-laws of the corporation. '

'Against the bye-laws, Officer? I had no idea. I am sorry. I'll move the equipment away at once.'

They all looked a bit confused and then the beachmaster said, 'Didn't know. Of course he knew. I told him over and over again.'

'I must have misunderstood,' I said. 'I'm so sorry, Officer.'

The two policemen looked at each other. I saw the suspicion of a wink.

'We shall have to report the case, sir. If any offence has been committed you may be hearing further from us. Of course if a complaint is made by the corporation, it may be the subject of a summons, sir.'

'I understand, Officer,' I said.

'In the meantime, sir, I must ask you to move this vehicle. You are committing a parking offence.'

I secured the 'dozer to the ring bolts on the loader, Julie climbed into the cab and we drove off. Soon we were out of the town and rumbling up the main road towards Lewes.

'You've done it, Sam,' Julie said. 'It's incredible, wonderful. I knew you'd do it.'

'We haven't quite done it yet, darling. She's not off yet.'

'But she will be, Sam. Nothing can stop her now.'

'I'd like to know who told the beachmaster,' I said. 'He must have known what we were up to or he wouldn't have put that barricade up at the top of the ramp. I don't know, but I've certainly got my suspicions.'

Julie put her hand over my hand as it rested on the gear lever.

'Sam, don't let's start arguing now. Forget about it, darling. Everything's gone well and everything's going to be all right. Let's not bother ourselves with that now, Sam. It's in the past, forget it—to please me, Sam.'

I said, 'All right, darling,' and kept quiet.

We arrived at the yard sharp on half past five. The manager was the only person there except for the taxi, which was waiting for us at the gate.

'Everything all right?' he asked.

'Yes, everything's fine.'

'Hope you got the garden dug all right.'

THIRTEEN

Julie and I got back to the Promenade in the taxi just before
six o'clock, as the dusk was beginning to close in. I saw at
once that Jake had connected up the wire to the winch and to
the *Rustler*'s stern. Now she stood at the head of a wide, deep
ditch leading to the sea. The wire from her stern lay on the
exposed sand at the bottom of the ditch and plumb in the
middle of it. There was no doubt that if nothing went wrong
now, she would have to come off. I sniffed the weather sus-
piciously. The rain had stopped and there was no more than a
light breeze from the west. It didn't look fine, but on the other
hand it didn't look too nasty. I wished we still had the radio
to get the shipping forecast. I was a fool not to have bought
another. I looked at my watch. It was ten to six.

'Listen, Julie, you go on board. I'm going to the café to
see if I can get the shipping forecast on their radio.

The taxi had gone but it wasn't far to the café. I sprinted
along the Promenade, across the road and arrived at the
'S.P.O.—Chips' at five to six. Horatia and Nelson were both
behind the bar serving coffee from the steaming machine. John
was sitting in the corner with a cup of tea. The girl with the
rat-tail hair was with him and two others I had seen on the
beach. The radio was on a high shelf behind the bar. It was
tuned to Luxembourg, blaring out the latest pop hit for all it
was worth.

'Do you mind if I listen to your radio?' I said to Nelson.
'I want to hear the weather forecast.'

'Help yourself, mate,' he said.

I went behind the bar, reached up to the knobs and started to tune the radio to the Light Programme. One of John's friends got up and came over.

'Here, wait a minute,' he said. 'I was listening to that—we all were.' He grabbed my arm. 'Who the hell do you think you are?' he said. 'Come off it.'

'I'm sorry,' I said, 'but it's important. I just want the forecast.'

'Bugger the forecast,' he shouted. 'Leave the bloody thing where it was.'

Then Horatia came up. ''Ere, we don't want any trouble 'ere,' she said. 'You leave it be and clear orf from be'ind this bloody bar. We're trying to serve customers.'

I was defeated. The time ticked by, the forecast came and went.

'Bloody nerve,' Nelson said as I went outside.

John came running out after me, 'Bad luck,' he said, 'those bloody people think of nothing but pop,' and then he said, 'Did you get the shingle cleared away?'

I said, 'Yes, I did. We're going off on the tide tonight,' and walked back towards the *Rustler*, leaving him on the pavement.

'I'll see you later,' he shouted after me. 'I want to see Julie before you go off.'

I didn't answer.

When I got back to the *Rustler* it was almost dark. Mr Pell and old Harry were on board, in the cabin, talking to Julie and Jake.

'Evening, Sam,' Mr Pell said as I came on board. 'You've made a lovely job of this—I never thought you'd manage it. Certainly never thought to see it done so neat. I reckon she'll come off a treat.'

Harry said, 'She'll come orf right enough, no doubt about that. 'E's dug right down to the sand you see with that there machinery—like it used to be before they built them groynes and brought all this bloody shingle up. Not a bit o' use interfering wi' nature, that's what I say.'

141

Julie said, 'Did you get the forecast, Sam?'

'No I couldn't get it. It was on the wrong station and they wouldn't let me change it.'

Mr Pell said, 'Don't worry about that, Sam. You can phone that number that's in the blue book—they'll give you a forecast. I remember your father always used to do that, Missie.'

'Of course we can,' Julie said. 'Silly not to think of it.'

Mr Pell said, 'I've got a berth ready for you, Sam. Same one as you had before. The chap I'd promised it to never turned up after all. It's been empty ever since you left it. I came over to tell you to go back into that berth, in case I'm not there tomorrow. I must go and catch my bus,' and Mr Pell went off down the ladder.

Old Harry said, 'I reckon it's going to blow all right. If you're lucky, you'll be clear before it starts. That old glass is a tumblin' down.'

I thanked Harry again for his knowledge about the winch and the anchor.

'It's thanks to you she's pretty well placed now,' I said.

'That's all right, young man,' he said. 'It's nice for us old'uns to be a bit of use to somebody now and then.'

Jake went off to take Harry home for his tea and to have his own.

'Come back at eleven, Jake,' I said to him. 'That'll give us a full hour before the tide in case anything crops up.'

'All right, Sam, I'll probably be back before that.'

Jake and I had been over every detail of what was to be done. Julie would be on board with me while Jake wound the winch. He would wind her out until she was over the block on Harry's anchor, then I would shout for him to stop. I would pick up the bridle over the stern and let go the shackle, allowing it to drop into the sea. Then she would swing round, bows out and stern to the beach on another rope that was already in position—from the eye of the wire to the bow. I would haul up on this rope until I got to the wire. Julie would start the engine and we would slip and be off. We would be in Newhaven inside a couple of hours. I arranged to meet Jake on the beach on Sunday morning to load all the gear into Mr Davis's truck. Jake and Harry went off and we heard their footsteps crunch across the gravel.

Julie said, 'Oh Sam, it was all for nothing. Did you hear what Mr Pell said about the berth? We could have stayed where we were. How dreadful.'

'Don't worry about what's happened, Julie. It's in the past like you said. Forget it.'

Julie made us some hot soup and we sat in the quiet, one on either side of the cabin table. We had a couple of hours to wait until Jake would come back and another hour before the tide was high. We were both pretty tired. It had been quite a day. We had been wet with the continuous rain but now we had changed our clothes and were comfortable again.

'It's been a battle, Sam,' Julie said, 'a real old battle.'

She put her hand on my knee underneath the table and looked at me with her great round eyes, 'Do you still love me, Sam? Really love me?'

'Why, of course, what's the matter, Julie?'

'Well, it's all been my fault, Sam, from beginning to end. It was my fault we left Newhaven, it was me who broke the engine, it was because of me that we came to this awful place. And I've been thinking, Sam, when I've been alone at night in that wretched hotel, I think I was wrong about John. I don't want to talk about it, Sam, or even think about it any more. I love John, we spent all our childhood together after all, and I did promise Dad I'd look after him. I just couldn't bring myself to believe anything so horrible about him, Sam, but now, since that business with the beachmaster this afternoon, I think I was wrong. Can you really forgive me for all this, Sam?'

I said, 'When you love someone—well, you love them don't you? It doesn't really make much difference what they do, you just go right on loving them. I suppose when you've been with a person for years and years you take it all for granted. I suppose if someone is mean, you might stop loving them, but you've never been mean to me. Besides, the things that have happened to us weren't your fault, they just happened. I think I understand about John now. I didn't at first but I do now and I don't think you could help that either. I do love you Julie, more than anything, more than life itself.'

She said, 'You've made me feel better, Sam. Thanks.'

It started raining again, this time quite hard. I was worried about the weather. With no radio and no barometer, I hadn't any idea what was happening, but it looked like another depression coming in. If we were going to have a bad night, I'd like to know what was in store. I looked up the number of the Met. Office in the Nautical Almanac. It was Bracknell 20242.

'I'm going ashore to telephone for a weather report.'

'I'll come with you,' she said, at once. 'It's only across the Promenade. We won't be gone ten minutes.'

We climbed into oilskins and walked to the telephone box. There was someone making a call and we stood waiting out of the rain in a doorway.

Then Julie said, 'Sam, I've just remembered something. I never paid the hotel bill. I think I'll run up and do it now and have a bath while I'm there. They won't mind and I feel a bit shivery and grubby.'

I gave her some money and said, 'You can go if you promise to come back, and if you give me a kiss.'

'All right,' she said, 'I'll do both those things,' and she kissed me with her soft mouth. 'I won't be more than an hour.'

'That means an hour and a half,' I said, 'but not a minute longer, Julie.'

'All right, Sam,' and she disappeared round a corner.

I waited in the rain for a chubby girl to finish her conversation. I dialled the Met. Office, put my money in the box and asked for extension 2508. After a couple of minutes I got through to the duty officer. Yes, there was a depression in the Atlantic moving slowly north-east. There were gale warnings for sea areas Portland and Plymouth and the wind would reach force seven or eight during the night in Wight, Dover and Thames. There would be rain for most of the night, clearing in the morning, moderate to good visibility.

I walked slowly back to the *Rustler* in the rain. I was tired, sick to death of struggling, with people, with the beach, with the bloody weather, with every contrary circumstance that had cast a blight on everything I had tried to do. Maybe I wasn't good at people—perhaps the people who seemed to be against me, like John and the beachmaster and Nelson, were reacting in some strange way against some arrogance in me, which I was not aware of. Anyway, I was tired. As soon as we got the *Rustler* safely back in Mr Pell's yard, I'd have a real rest—do nothing but sleep and eat and make love for a week. As I came to the Promenade, the *Rustler* made a bare, bleak outline through the rain and the night. It would have been nice to have had some decent weather, tonight of all nights. It had been lovely for a fortnight but now it had gone sour on me—like everything else. I was in a mood of depression for no reason I could pinpoint. The balance of the mind is a delicate mechanism, swinging without motive between ecstasy and a cheerless, neurotic despondency. When a man is at the end of his tether, the mind can slip away from what is rational and acceptable—sometimes into blind and senseless violence. The borders of insanity are ill-defined.

As I got near the boat I saw someone climb the ladder and go on board—that would be Jake, back from his tea earlier than I expected—odd that I hadn't seen him walking down the beach in front of me. I had my foot on the bottom rung of the ladder when I felt myself become aware of a thought, an idea, a sudden apprehension. It sent a wave of shivers down my spine. Maybe it wasn't Jake on board. I walked very quietly towards the stern, running my hand along the rope sling which we had put round the *Rustler*. When I got near the shackle, I felt it. The rope was cut—almost right through so that it hung only on a strand—and the cut was bound over with tape so that the strands of the rope should not run back. I moved my hand round through the shackle and up to the other part of the sling. There was another cut, identical to the first one and bound over with tape in the same way. It was neatly done. As soon as the strain came on it, the bridle would break in two places, the wire would spring back into the sea and be lost.

I felt a wave of anger which flushed through my body like a red rash. It was as if I had been injected with some drug which made my muscles tighten and contract, the skin over my face draw tight, the blood flowed through my veins like a river in flood. At the same time I felt a strength in me that had never been there before, inspired by a force which was outside my control. I went up the ladder. John was in the cabin sitting at the table writing a note, on the top page of a block I always kept on the chart table. There was a pile of his belongings on the table— a small bag I had seen him with before, his tin of grass and a box of matches. Beside them was a roll of adhesive tape. He stood up when he saw me and scooped the bag on to the bunk behind him.

'You bastard,' I said, 'you bastard, this is the finish of you.'

I went into the cabin and seized him round the throat. I don't believe I had any control over what I was doing. I squeezed his neck and shook him like a rat. His shifty eyes were staring. His head wobbled like the head of a rag doll. His legs seemed to give under him so that I was holding him up by his thin, soft neck. A stream of saliva dribbled out of a corner of his contorted mouth.

'Julie,' he croaked, 'let me see Julie.'

I let go of him and he dropped down on to the bunk. He put his hands up to his throat and looked at me. Perhaps it was the pathetic, animal look on his face that made me release my grip, or perhaps it was the words he spoke—I don't know. I felt the force inside me begin to ebb away, leaving me shaking and trembling and suddenly weak.

'I nearly murdered you. I'm sorry.'

He was all collapsed, a weak and worthless bag of utterly contemptible skin and bone.

'I'm sorry I didn't murder you. It would have been the best thing for you.'

He recovered himself quickly, more quickly than I recovered myself. John never lacked courage in a strange sort of way.

'I did it for Julie,' he said hoarsely. 'I only did it for her. I don't care about you, only about her. You're ruining her. You're wrecking her career and now you're taking her away to live in squalor with a bloody labourer. You can do what you like to me, Sam, but as long as I live I'll go on trying to get Julie away from you. You don't frighten me. I'd rather die than see Julie tied to you for ever.'

I picked up the little cloth bag and looked inside. There was a small bottle full of tablets, heroin I supposed. There was a hypodermic syringe and there were the bunches of car keys.

'Quite a stock in trade,' I said.

I felt calm again. I felt a profound relief that I had not gone on shaking him until his neck broke or until he choked to death.

'Just one or two things to get the record straight, John.' I gave him a sharp push and he slumped against the back of the settee. He was as pale as death, his hands still feeling round his throat. 'You just tell me the truth and I'll leave your neck alone—a little bargain between friends.'

He said nothing, only looked at me with his shifty eyes.

'First of all, how did you snarl up the anchor, John?'

At first he said nothing. I moved a step towards him.

'Keep your bloody hands off me. I let out some chain and then swam down and hitched it over the fluke.'

'And the dinghy—where did you put the dinghy?'

'Along the beach. I brought it back when you were asleep—after she drove up. I was watching the whole thing.'

'And our things—the binoculars, the clock, the rope—what happened to them?'

He was silent again.

'Come on, John, you'll feel better when you've got all this out of your system.'

'I got thirty quid for them, from a chap I know.'

'Enough to keep you going for a week or so I suppose. You're a sticker, aren't you. So then you told the beachmaster about the bulldozer and after that failed, you only had one trick left. Well, bad luck, John. Jake will be down in an hour or so. It won't take us long to make a new sling.'

I looked at the note he had been writing—It said, 'Dear Julie, I'm off to London in the morning. I'll get in touch with you in a week's time ...' I screwed it up and put it in my pocket.

'Charming little note for your sister. Then I suppose a quick fix under the pier, all very nice. But I'm afraid you've lost, John. You've failed. You tried hard but you've failed. Even if you had wrecked the *Rustler*, you would still have failed, because there's something about life you don't understand. Perhaps it's not your fault but you don't understand it. You see, John, when two people are in love, like Julie and I are in love, it's stronger than you, stronger than anything. I think it would be better if you left us for a time. My friend Inspector Parks will be interested in this lot. He'll be interested in that little bag of yours. Now, get in the fo'castle. I'm going to lock the door and I'm going to fetch the police. They can do what they like with you. At least, they'll keep you out of my hair for a year or so.'

He went into the fo'castle quite meekly and with a certain dignity I couldn't help admiring, taking with him his tin of grass and the box of matches. I slid the door shut, dropped the hasp over the ring and secured it with the spike out of my belt.

I heard him say, 'You'll regret this, Sam. I swear to God you'll regret this.'

I went ashore at once, up the ramp, and along towards the police station. I'd get this business settled first. Jake and I would still have time to make a new bridle before the tide came up. The brute anger in me had turned to a blind bitterness. In my agitation, I was acting without thinking, doing the first thing that came into my head without pause for proper consideration. Julie wouldn't like it—well, she'd have to like it. John was a menace, not only to me but to everyone, including himself. I didn't see that with all its imperfections, society ought to have to carry John along. He ought to be cured or locked up. Maybe they'd send him to some sort of clinic and do him some good. I didn't know what they did with drug addicts and I didn't much care as long as they took him somewhere where he couldn't interfere with me. The police station was quiet. There was only one constable in the reception office, sitting on a high stool at the big desk, reading a magazine.

'Can I see Inspector Parks, Officer?'

'He's not here, sir. He's off duty—won't be in till Monday morning. He's got the weekend off.'

It hadn't entered my head that the inspector wouldn't be there. I was a bit taken aback.

'Oh, all right, Officer. It wasn't anything important. I'll call and see him later.'

I went outside, crossed the road, sat on a seat in a small park near the police station and tried to think sensibly. It would have been easy if the inspector had been there, but it would take hours of explaining to start the whole thing off from scratch. Besides, Julie would be terribly hurt if I went to the police without even telling her. I ought to see her first and tell her what had happened. She'd be back on board in a few minutes anyway. I looked at my watch, she'd been away over an hour now. If she came back on board and found the boat full of policemen and John and the drugs and everything, it would be dreadful. I was a fool not to have waited until she came, a bloody fool. Of course, that would have been the right thing to have done. I walked quickly to the hotel to meet her before she went back to the *Rustler*.

'Miss Cranbrook?' the porter said. 'She left about a quarter of an hour ago.'

I ran through the rain as fast as I could.

For a moment, what I saw when I reached the Promenade didn't connect to my senses. My mind was working its way through a profound confusion brought on, perhaps, by the surge of anger which had overcome me. Half-formed ideas flowed in and out of my brain like waves on a beach so that when I was faced with the reality of a disaster I found myself unable to comprehend it. I stood on top of the Promenade like a man in a dream, watching with a sort of fascinated curiosity as smoke poured out of the *Rustler*'s companionway and as the crimson fire lit the skylights and the porthole in the sleeping cabin with a brilliant, golden light. It was John of course. He must have set the boat on fire. The fo'castle was full of inflammable things—rags, flares, sails, blankets, rope—which would only have to be soaked in paraffin to go up like a firework. Poor bastard. He'd come to the end of everything. His own funeral pyre would be his revenge. And then, suddenly, the understanding came to me that I myself was a part of this scene, that Julie was probably on board, that when the flames reached the petrol cans by the mast everything connected with the *Rustler* would be wiped away in one final conflagration. The inertia left me and was replaced by wild and uncontrollable energy. I raced down the ramp and across the beach, tripping and stumbling in the dark against the ruts and mounds of shingle that had been left by the bulldozer. I flung myself at the ladder and stumbled to the top.

Julie was stretched out on the cabin floor. Her clothes were on fire—she seemed to be enveloped in flames. The marlin spike was in her hand, the fo'castle door was open and a wall of flame, dancing and spluttering and reaching out its curling, twisting fingers was already invading the saloon and seeking out the tins of petrol by the mast with evil accuracy. Julie saw me for an instant through the smoke. She raised her head and for an anguished moment I looked into those dark eyes.

I saw her lips move, saw them frame the words and heard her cry, 'Sam, for the love of God, John's in there.'

Then she lost consciousness.

For some reason that I do not fully understand, I found myself able to think clearly when faced with the reality of a desperate situation. There were no intangibles here to confuse and harass, only a straightforward problem that would respond to a straightforward remedy. The *Rustler* was well equipped with fire extinguishers. I took the one from inside the companionway near the engine and sprayed the liquid indiscriminately over Julie, over the petrol cans and to the base of the fire through the fo'castle door. Then I moved for'ard through the dense smoke, took the second extinguisher from its place by the door to the sleeping cabin and advanced into the fo'castle itself. The heat was intense but the extinguishers quelled the flames quickly. Through the smoke, I saw John slumped on the bench. I made sure the fire was completely out. I put my hand inside John's jacket. He was badly burned —his face was an unrecognizable mask of livid and distorted flesh—but he was alive. I carried his frail frame into the saloon and laid him on the starboard settee.

Then I heard Jake's voice on the ladder, 'Sam, are you there? Is everything all right?'

'Listen, Jake, there's been a fire on board. John's badly burned and so is Julie. Go to the telephone box, call an ambulance and wait on the Promenade until it comes. Tell them to hurry.'

I lifted Julie on to the other settee. She turned towards me and opened her eyes. Her head and shoulders were horribly burned. Her brown hair was gone on one side. I gave her some brandy in a glass.

'Is John alive?'

'Yes, he's over there. He's alive.'

'You swear it, Sam?'

'Yes, I swear it. Jake's phoning the ambulance. They'll be here in a minute.'

She said, 'I saw the fire and heard him scream. When I opened the door the flames and the heat threw me back. I tried to reach him, Sam, but it was too hot for me. I didn't think of the extinguisher, Sam, just didn't think of it.'

She was quiet for a few minutes. I knelt beside her as she

lay on the settee and we looked into each other's eyes. The tears rolled down our cheeks in four uncontrollable streams.

She said, 'Sam, how did John get in there? How did he get locked in?'

I said, 'Leave it till later. I'll explain it all to you, later.'

She said, 'No, Sam, tell me now. It's important—I must know.'

I said, 'He tried to wreck us again. I caught him cutting the bridle. I locked him in and went to get Inspector Parks but he wasn't there, so I went to the hotel but I missed you. I came back and saw the fire.'

Then we heard the ambulance men coming across the shingle and Jake's voice as they lifted the stretchers up the ladder.

Julie said, 'Sam, promise me one thing?'

She spoke slowly. I could see through the dim light that she was struggling with the words, fighting to remain conscious until she could get them out.

'Save the *Rustler*, Sam. Get her off this beach tonight, Sam. Don't worry about me. Save the *Rustler*. She's our happiness.'

And then she fainted and the ambulance men took her and John away.

FOURTEEN

It was eleven o'clock and the tide was already flooding up through the channel I had cleared across the beach. It was already blowing from the west but the rain had stopped. You could hear the rising wind singing through the *Rustler*'s rigging and the waves were already crashing on the beach. I knew that the gale would flatten our feeble excavations in the shingle. It was our last chance to get the *Rustler* off. Maybe even now the sea would level the beach before we could get her through to deep water. We had less than one hour. The odds, once more, were against us—Jake and I battling by ourselves against a gale. It seemed that we were always against the elements, that they were never on our side. It was a familiar pattern—matching our inadequate strength against forces which dwarfed us—only this time it would be Jake and I by ourselves instead of Julie and I.

Jake was seething with curiosity.

'What happened, Sam?' he said as we walked quickly towards the *Rustler*. 'How did she catch fire?'

'Listen, Jake, I swear I'll tell you the whole story tomorrow but right now, we've got a hell of a lot to do in a short time. Be a friend and don't ask me to explain now.'

In the dark I took him to the stern and showed him the damaged bridle with a torch. He whistled through his teeth.

'Run back the winch and get some slack on the cable. Then unshackle it and we'll repair the bridle. Secure the end of the cable so you don't lose it.'

Already the sea was round the *Rustler*'s stern. The steep, fierce little waves that I knew so well were already breaking round our legs. I ran on board. The coil of rope we had used for the bridle was stowed in the fo'castle. Useless, it would have been burned or at least damaged by the fire. There was a mooring warp in one of the cockpit lockers. I dragged it out and dropped it down on the shingle, picked up my spike from the cabin sole where Julie had dropped it, and went down the ladder. Jake already had the shackle off the bridle. We cut through the rope in the two places where John had already damaged it and made a long bowline in each side of the bridle. Jake did the port side and I did the other. Now we were working up to our waists in water. The tide was flooding fast. Then we cut down the mooring warp and threaded it from one bowline to the other round the *Rustler*'s stern until we had made enough parts to give it the same strength as the rest of the bridle. Lastly, struggling to keep our balance against the waves, we made fast the wire to the bridle once again. The *Rustler* was already beginning to move under the impact of the waves.

'You'll just have to turn that bloody handle like hell, Jake, and hope for the best. Christ knows whether she'll come. I'll be on board.'

I had that same sick feeling in the pit of my stomach that I had had the last time when Julie and I tried and failed to get the *Rustler* off Brighton beach. The arrangements I had made—the rope sling, the winch, the wire out to old Harry's block—were all very well and were logical enough, given reasonable conditions. But in a gale everything is different. The wind can make a mockery of a well laid plan, can reduce order to perverse chaos. I looked at my watch.

'We'll get the sheerlegs off her now.'

The *Rustler* was feeling the water round her. The waves were slapping up under her stern and causing her to jerk and quiver as she had done before. Jake and I moved the ladder up to the bow and went on board. The wind was pressing her on to the starboard leg. We went to the portside, threw off the lashings, lifted the heavy baulk of timber clear and threw it down on the shingle. She began to move from side to side, banging gently against the remaining, starboard sheerleg. Then we heard a shout from the beach.

The beachmaster was standing on the shingle near the bow, dressed in his black oilskin suit. His baby face was turned up towards us, reflecting the lights from the Promenade, the golden hair curled up round the bottom of his hat.

'Mr Pickson, sir,' he shouted.

I looked at Jake.

'What the hell's the matter now?' he said.

We both went down the ladder.

'What is it, beachmaster? What's wrong now?'

'Ah, Mr Pickson, sir,' he said. 'Well, sir, the fact is, sir ... what I was going to say sir, was ...'

'Come on, beachmaster,' I said. 'We're in a hurry. What's the matter?'

And then he came out with it, 'Nothing untoward, sir, but I heard about the young lady, sir, and about the fire, sir. The ambulance driver, he's a relation of my wife. I thought, sir ... well, I thought you might like a hand, like some help, seeing you're one short.'

I looked at him in astonishment.

'By Christ, beachmaster, you're a bloody hero. I'll say I'd like some help. You can turn the winch with Jake,' and I shook him by the hand. 'I'll take the other sheerleg off, Jake. Start turning as soon as I give you the word.'

The starboard sheerleg was not as easy to get clear as the port one had been. The wind had risen to gale force now. The *Rustler* was almost afloat and her whole weight was pressed against the heavy timber. I cut away the lashings, but I wasn't strong enough to lift it clear. Oh well, it would have to clear itself.

I shouted, 'All right, beachmaster, turn. Turn like hell.'

I saw the two of them bend to the winch and felt the strain

come on the bridle. Now the waves were crashing against the *Rustler*'s side and she was beginning to lift again and bang on the shingle. I saw the cable come taut, heard the creaks and groans as the rope bridle took the strain and suddenly the *Rustler* began to move backwards.

She lifted and banged down on the shingle just as she had before and each time she lifted she moved slowly astern, perhaps a foot at a time. I saw the two of them turning the winch, the handles flying round as she came astern, and then I saw them straining with all their strength until she lifted again and moved another foot towards the sea. I saw the sheerleg fall away and drift clear. Now the wind was pressing her against the shingle bank of the trench, she was heeled right over and being dragged through the shingle on her side, pressed down by the wind, lifting and banging, her masts and rigging shaking with each concussion, her whole frame racked by this brutality as it had been before.

'Oh you poor bloody old boat,' I shouted at her. 'This must stop soon.'

It did stop. Suddenly she came free of the beach and swung her stern to the wind. She swung parallel to the shore but with her stern pointing towards the West pier, securely fastened by the wire to the block on the bottom. Jake and the beachmaster stopped turning and she lay pitching her stern into the waves, spray flying over her and sometimes the green tops of the seas rolling over the after part and into the cockpit. I looked carefully round. I could see Jake and the beachmaster standing by the winch and I could see that there was enough room for her to swing. There was a strong warp from the bow already in position, down the starboard side, outside everything and fast to the eye of the wire. All I had to do was to let go the shackle and she would turn right round and lie with her bow towards the wind instead of her stern. Then I could cut the bridle free and allow it to drop down, hoist sail and away. As luck would have it she still had the reefs tied in the mains'l.

I went into the cabin to get a safety harness—it would do

156

no good to fall overboard. I hadn't been into the cabin since the fire. I had almost forgotten about the fire—all that was in my mind was Julie's burnt face as she lay on the cabin settee and her words, 'Save the *Rustler*, Sam—she's our happiness.' The fo'castle was a charred shell. Almost everything in it was gone —sails, rope, stores of every kind were no longer there. The paint was all scorched and blistered and all the orderly racks and piles of gear were nothing but charred heaps of burnt dust. Only the main frames of the ship had escaped serious damage. My safety harness, always kept on a brass hook just inside the fo'castle door, was gone except for the metal fastenings.

I shrugged, 'Just hold on tight—that's all.'

I had to lean right out over the stern to get at the shackle— stretch myself along the bumkin, balancing with my feet hooked over the afterdeck, hanging on with one hand to the mizzen boom. I hadn't bargained for a gale. In the weather I had banked on, I would have been able to draw the wire inboard, ease the strain and let the shackle go but now everything was bar tight. I wasn't strong enough to get slack on the wire with the *Rustler*'s weight and windage hanging on to it. By stretching out I reached the shackle with my spike and began to turn laboriously, half a turn at a time. Slowly the pin came out of the shackle until only half a turn of thread was left. I looked behind me and towards the shore. The waves were crashing on the beach, seas were breaking over me as I clung to the bumkin, but there was room for her to swing. I undid the last half-turn with the spike. There was a bang as the wire sprung back, the strain came on the rope and the *Rustler* began to turn.

I thought I had done everything right. Jake and I had made the bridle as strong as we knew how. The rope that would swing her round was strong and it was properly fast at both ends. I had thought through this operation a hundred times from start to finish, anticipating every conceivable thing that could go wrong, guarding against every mischance, however remote. Still I had done it wrong—not Jake—myself with my own hand. *Rustler* swung halfway round as I climbed back into the cockpit, and there she hung, broadside to the wind and the seas. She was heeling over to port at a horrible angle, the seas were hitting her exposed flank and sending up columns of spray, the water was up her lee deck and was pouring through the hatch. I clung to the weather lifeline in the cockpit in a daze. What in the name of Jesus had gone wrong? And then I realized the thing I had done with my own hand. In the dark, when I had tied the bowline on the bridle—the bowline I had tied when Jake and I repaired John's malicious damage—I had tied it over the top of the bow warp instead of underneath it so that now, instead of swinging clear when the *Rustler* turned, it was caught up amidships. Now the bridle, bar tight round the hull and out of my reach, was holding her athwart the seas. She would sink in minutes, unless, unless I could free the wire.

I climbed up the sloping deck to the weather side and looked towards the beach. I could see the dim outlines of Jake and the beachmaster standing side by side on the shore.

'Slack out wire,' I shouted. 'Let the wire run off the winch.'

There was no chance that they could hear my words. They were snatched away by the wind and scattered to leeward with the flying spray and the spume. I waved and shouted and shouted and waved but the pair of them stood there by the water's edge, like cold, uncomprehending statues. Why couldn't that bloody beachmaster understand? He'd been in the Navy hadn't he? Surely he had some intelligence in him. Hadn't he been a signalman? And then I knew what to do. I climbed to the companionway—the water was pouring in every time a sea hit her—reached to the ledge above the chart table and found my torch. Then I climbed back to the stern and flashed in morse.

'Let go the wire. Let it run off the winch.'

It took a minute to send the message and at once I saw them run back to the winch. Jake knew how to work the brake mechanism and the clutch. She'd be free in moments.

I climbed along the sloping deck letting go the sail tyers as I went. The gaff fell off to leeward and the sail got wind under it and began to flap and shake. I heaved on the halyards and slowly the mains'l climbed up the mast and filled with wind. I heaved on the topping lift and the boom lifted off the gallows. Then I let go the tyer on the jib and heaved on the halyard. She was moving ahead now. The wire had gone slack. I couldn't see it now but I knew that she was still fast to it. She was no longer pinned down. She must be dragging the whole bloody thing across the bottom. The bare end would run out through the sheave in old Harry's block and the whole thing would be dragging behind like a trawl. I came aft to the wheel and steadied her. She was making leeway. The wire and the bridle under her were dragging her back so that she was going as fast sideways as she was going ahead, towards the Palace Pier. I could see the light on the end of the Palace Pier and I could see she wasn't going to weather it. Only one thing could save her from smashing herself to pieces. She needed the stays'l, she needed power. The engine was useless. With ropes round the bottom of the hull like a cat's cradle the propeller would foul at once. With the stays'l she just might weather the end of the pier. I went below with the torch to get it, and then I realized it wasn't there. The stays'l, all the spare sails, had gone. There was nothing but ashes in their place. I looked again at the pier. Now I could see the structure to leeward. I could see the crisscross iron and I could see the seas crashing against it. I pressed the starter button and slammed the engine into gear. It was the last thing I could do. After that I had no more ideas, no further resources.

The engine roared into life. When I put it in gear it ran for a few moments and then it stopped dead, as I knew it must. I supposed I would be able to get into the latticework of the pier while the *Rustler* smashed herself to matchwood, cling to it like a monkey, cling to life itself. One had to live, after all. Julie wanted me. Maybe now, after what had happened, she would need me more. Then I looked to leeward and suddenly

I saw that the *Rustler* had picked herself up and had begun to sail. I looked along the lee side and saw the water rushing past, looked up at the pier, only yards away, and saw that she was sailing away from it. The light at the end was under her lee and she was sailing past it and out into the open sea.

At first I couldn't believe it but in a few minutes the pier was behind me, the lights of Brighton were back in their rightful place along the horizon, the noise of Brighton and the smell of Brighton were gone. I eased the sheet, the *Rustler* payed off the wind and began to race towards Newhaven with a bone in her mouth and a rising gale behind her. That strange quality of luck that I find it so hard to believe in had, for once, worked to our advantage, turning a situation of hopelessness to our favour, making a disaster into a triumph at a single stroke of the divine providence. In fouling the rope bridle the engine had jerked it clear of the hull and the weight of the wire had dragged it to the bottom, at the same time freeing the turn round the propeller. Such are the twists of fortune that restore a man's faith.

I took the mains'l off her when the light on the pier at Newhaven was close aboard, started the engine and ran into the harbour under jib. I berthed alongside in the outer harbour at half past two, using the jib sheets and the stays'l sheets for warps and walked to the telephone box on the quay.

I spoke to the ward sister. 'How is Miss Cranbrook?'

'She's comfortable but she's asleep. I'm sorry but she can't be disturbed.'

'How is her brother, Mr John Cranbrook?'

'I'm sorry. He died soon after he was admitted.'

'Will you please give Miss Cranbrook a message when she wakes up? Tell her that the *Rustler* is home, that the *Rustler* is safe.'